Ignite My Fire

Copyright

Opening Quote

She's like standin' in the rain. Washes all my cares away. At the end of a long, hot day, she's like standin' in the rain.
She gets on you, under your skin like a tattoo. She'll always be there. She holds on, stuck in your head like an old song. She ain't goin' nowhere

Starin' At The Sun by Jason Aldean

Chapter One

☿ Lila ☿

One year.

Exactly.

That's how long it's been since Daniel came into my life and turned my world upside down. He swept me off my feet like some modern day Prince Charming and has been sweeping me off my feet every single day since. Like I'm his very own Cinderella.

Well, okay. I'm not really Cinderella. My family is amazing. But *Cinderella* is my all time favorite Disney movie. I love everything about it, though so many in this day and age disagree. How could someone so in love not recognize the love of his life? Why would he have to use a slipper to tell who she is? No one falls in love in an hour.

Excuse me, but it's a fairytale. It's full of magic and wonder. Why can't people just lose themselves in the story and allow themselves to be a kid again? Is it so awful to dream of one's own fairytale story in their own life?

That's what I thought.

So, when Daniel dropped into my life and swept me up into our very own fairytale, I let him. Why wouldn't I? Everyone deserves to have a love like Prince Charming and Cinderella. Their very own happily ever after.

I turn down the street to his house giddy for what's to come. It's our anniversary. Over the past six months of our relationship, we've been spending more and more time together. So much so that I've moved quite a bit of my stuff into his house. He keeps telling me that I make it more of a home to him. He hasn't felt that way since he inherited it from his grandparents a few years ago. Even after he spent so much time remodeling it with his bare hands.

I'm just happy that I've been able to make it feel like a home to him. Finally. He deserves it. Daniel is so amazing. He's only twenty-four and already runs his own company. It's a general contractor company, and he loves it. He doesn't like building from the ground up. He's a big fan of remodeling what's already been given and making it more beautiful.

My smile widens as I near his house. He certainly has the body of a contractor. He's six feet. Like me, he has light brown hair and hazel eyes. But compared to me, he's a giant. I'm petite. Really rather small. I've been described as a dainty Southern Belle. If only they really knew me. He has muscles in all of the right places that have been built from hard work. I've never seen him spend a day in the gym, but I doubt he needs to.

I pull into his driveway and stare up at his house, grinning from ear to ear. It's two stories. It's one of the older homes in our smallish town of ten-thousand. It looks a little like that old plantation house that Melanie Carmicheal is obsessed with in that movie, *Sweet Home Alabama*. For the record, I'm so in love with Reese Witherspoon. That girl is incredible and so talented.

I excitedly get out of my black, convertible Mustang. New, obviously. Who honestly likes those old ones before 2010 anyway? I mean, seriously? Eew.

Okay, not eew. I know someone who loves old cars. I'm pretty sure he built his car from the ground up. Actually, I know he did. I was there with him and his two best friends while he did it. It probably helped a lot that one of his best friends is my older brother, Keelan. Not that he ever drives the thing. He's said it himself. It's a death trap. He just likes working on it on his days off to give himself something to do. He's been tinkering with it for fourteen years.

I shake my head. He should be the last person I'm thinking of. I have someone in my life. Someone who notices me and pays attention. Someone who loves me and supports me. I don't need him. I have Daniel.

At the thought of my boyfriend, I let out a little squeal of excitement. I reach into the backseat and carefully pull out the pizza I had made especially for us. Thank goodness for local pizzerias. The pizza says 'Happy One Year Anniversary!' The words are spelled out in sausage, Daniel's favorite. The pizza is a little larger than usual, but it's shaped like a heart, and I love the way it turned out.

After I get the box out, I close the door.

And that's when I notice the strange car in the driveway. I furrow my brows and tilt my head. It's a baby blue Fiat. Daniel drives an old Dodge Ram. I stand for a few moments looking between the car and the house before finally swallowing hard and deciding to go inside.

The closer I get to the door, the harder my heart pounds. I tell myself I'm being stupid. There's a reasonable explanation for this. Maybe it's one of his friends. Maybe it's a relative. I nod. It's all innocent. Daniel wouldn't do anything to break my heart. I was putting our clothes away yesterday and saw a ring box in his drawer. I quickly put it away and pretended like I saw nothing.

Feeling a little better at the shock of seeing the strange car, I reach for the door handle. It's locked, but I'm not surprised. Daniel is extremely cautious. He was raised to be. His dad was a police officer in a neighboring town that's bigger than ours here in Piper Falls, Texas.

I fumble a little for my key and unlock the door, my excitement filling me once more. I can't wait to celebrate with him. We agreed to pizza, wine, and a movie. We're both the type who are perfectly content at home. Though, I did want to go out tonight. Aurora Heights would have been nice. It's a rooftop restaurant near the falls on the outskirts of town. The place is so special. Patrons can see the sky whether they're inside or outside. I've never been there, but I've always wanted to go. I've been hinting at it for weeks.

When I enter, it's quiet, and that sense of dread I felt outside befalls me once more. I look around with furrowed brows as I quietly close the door, but something keeps me from actually calling out. Something isn't right.

And then I hear it.

Panting.

Moaning.

The slapping of sweaty, wet skin against skin.

The bile rises in my throat, but I don't gag. Not until I turn the corner and see Daniel, *my Daniel*, on the couch with some bottle-blond bimbo with too much makeup and giant, fake boobs that are flapping up and down in Daniel's face. He doesn't seem to mind at all.

He grips her ass and slams her down on his dick over and over. His dick, the one I thought was only meant for me, is pounding into her again and again. The moans and grunts get louder and louder. I can't tear my eyes away. I'm in complete shock that this is happening right in front of me. This has to be a dream. There's no other explanation. I have to be in a state of sleep.

He's not even wearing a condom. He's fucked me with that cock with no condom. He's come inside me with no condom. I've been on birth control for years because of an irregular period. We talked before we had sex for the first time. I never thought my boyfriend, the one I trusted with all of me, could ever do something like this.

Anger radiates through my being as furious tears sting my eyes. Before I know what I'm doing, I'm opening the pizza box and throwing slices at both of them, pegging them both in the head, her on the back and ass, and him on the dick.

"Ah!" I scream in frustrated, heartbroken anger.

"What the fuck, Lila?" Daniel screams at me, throwing his bimbo off him and onto the couch. The same couch we've made love on. The same couch I've ridden him on just like she was.

"Ah!" the bimbo yells as she puts her hands up to her face. "Make her stop!"

"How could you! What the fuck is wrong with you?" I scream as I throw slice after slice of pizza at them both, hitting them both in the face and chest.

When I have no more pizza to throw, I throw the box at them and turn to flee. I'm barely aware of Daniel getting up and throwing on pants. I wipe my hands on my shirt and run to my car. Rage fuels me as I jump in. My purse is still snuggly strapped across my chest. I lock my doors from the inside when I see him running out after me.

"Lila! Open the fucking door!" Daniel orders as he tries to get my car door open.

"Get away from me!" I scream back at him as I dig for my keys. Finally finding them, I slam them into the ignition and start the engine. Tears blind me. I can hardly see, but I throw my car into reverse anyway.

"Lila! Stop it! Let me explain! Open the door!"

"Explain?" I squeak scream. "What happened, Daniel? She lost her memory, thought you were her husband, and you fucked her?"

"Lila! Open the door!" His eyes are burning with the same fiery fury that mine are, but he has another thing coming if he thinks I'm opening this door.

"Get away from me!" I stomp on the accelerator. My car rockets back out of the driveway. I turn at the last second, just before hitting a telephone pole.

Daniel is chasing me down the driveway. "Lila! Come on! Let's talk! I love you, baby!"

"Love? This is what you call love?" He can't hear me as I slam my car in drive and burn rubber out of there.

At the end of the block, I whip around the corner, barely acknowledging the yield sign. It isn't until I find myself near the fire station downtown, which is only a few blocks from Daniel's house, do I realize that I shouldn't be driving home. I shouldn't be driving at all. I'm so angry that my grip on the steering wheel is hurting my hands and making them cramp, but it's more the fact that tears bursting from my heart and leaking from my eyes are blurring my vision.

Keelan. He's working today, isn't he?

I need my brother.

I tear into the back parking lot of the fire station like a bat out of hell. I slam on my brakes after whipping into a parking spot near where the firefighters park their personal vehicles. One of the fire trucks is outside being cleaned. When I get out of my car, I realize that this isn't Keelan's crew.

Nick Carmichael, a well-built firefighter with dark hair and green eyes, glances at the others around him before dropping something in his hand into a bucket and walking towards me. From his back pocket, he grabs a shirt and puts it on.

"Lila? What's up, sweetheart?"

I sniffle and hug myself. "I was thinking Keelan was working today. I guess I got his schedule messed up." I turn towards my car, shaking my head. "I'll just call him."

"Hang on a second. What's going on? You look upset. And I hope that red shit on you is sauce of some sort and not blood."

I close my eyes as I turn slowly towards him again. I open them

8

after a few moments, but it's only because the images of Daniel and his bimbo screwing each other's brains out comes rushing back, making me want to claw out my mind's eye.

"Something happened. That's all." I look down at my hands and shirt. He's right. My shirt is stained with the pizza sauce I wiped on it from my hands.

Nick looks over his shoulder before looking back at me. "Cap is here. Why don't you come inside and call Keelan from the office?"

I just nod and let him lead me inside the station and to the Captain's office. Elden Falcon is Crew B's Captain. That's the crew Nick works on. I've known Elden my whole life. Just as I've known his brother.

Blake.

Blake would never have done this to me. He's too much of a man. If only he saw me the way I see him. I've been in love with him since I knew the meaning of the word. Hell, probably even before that.

But Blake is seven years older than me. He grew up with my brother. He's always seen me as his best friend's annoying little sister who followed them around everywhere they went and wanted to hang out when they were doing boy things.

Like building that '69 Corvette of his.

He always asked me why I liked hanging around and irritating the shit out of him. I obviously couldn't tell him it was because I thought he was hot. And the older I got, the hotter he became. I couldn't tell him that the first time I touched myself were to thoughts of him.

Yeah. Because that would make me sound like the mature woman he wanted and not the little girl he thinks I am. I roll my eyes at myself. Blake will never want me the way I do him. When Daniel came into my life, I thought it was my way to prove to myself there were other men out there. And it worked.

For a while.

Now that my retinas are burned with in living color photographs of who he really is beneath his pretty exterior and Prince Charming facade, Blake is back in my heart full force.

Yeah, right. Like he ever left.

Nick closes the door behind me after he lets me step into the Captain's office. Elden looks up. His eyes widen. "Fuck me, Lila." He stands and crosses the office to me. "What happened to you?"

As soon as his hands touch my arms, I break down in sobs. He wraps his arms around me and hugs me tight. He's whispering in my ear, but I can't even hear him. The tears are gut-wrenching this time. Powerful enough to shake my very being.

"H-how c-could h-he d-do th-this t-to m-me!" I wail into his chest as I grip his shirt.

"Okay, sweetie. Breathe for me now." He grips me tighter with one arm and reaches for something with the other. I don't care what it is. "Get here," he growls. And then like magic, that arm is around me once more.

Steadying me in the Texas tornado going on in my heart.

Shielding me from the rain lashing down on my soul.

Blake, my heart cries. *God, how I wish you were Blake.*

Elden holds me while I sob all the moisture in my body out; until I feel like I'm nothing but a shell. I don't know how long it is, but I'm just starting to calm when Keelan pulls me into his strong arms and sits down with me in his lap.

"What the hell happened to you, Lils?" he whispers in my ear. "What the fuck did that asshole do to you?" He hugs me close and tight until I'm finally relaxed enough to tell him everything.

Keelan has never liked Daniel. But he's never liked any of my boyfriends. I've always thought it was him being overprotective. I don't know why it took this long to see that every single time he's warned me about someone, he's been right. How could I have been so stupid and not listened to him?

The breakups before never mattered to me, though. I never cared about any of them because I couldn't let go of Blake. Daniel was the first one I allowed myself to really let go with. To allow myself to feel things with. And as soon as I started to do that, I started to get over Blake.

Only, I guess I really didn't because all I want right now is him.

"I'm taking you home," Keelan says.

"And then we're going to deal with that douche," a deep voice growls from behind me. My head snaps up to see Luke Bradley. He gives me a sweet smile. It's a smile no one really ever sees. He's another person I've known my whole life. I know he hates his smile. It's rare to see him not smirk. "I was with Keelan when you called."

I just nod as I stand. "I just want my stuff," I say quietly. "I have so much of it there."

"We'll take care of it," Keelan says as he stands. Much like Daniel, Keelan towers over me. He's six feet and muscular. Like a firefighter should be, I suppose. He's got the same color hair as me and the same hazel eyes.

Luke is a little taller. He has blue eyes, but he could probably pass for our brother. Growing up, many people thought he was our brother. The only one who really stood out from us all was Blake. He's always been tall and dark. Broody and quiet, but the silently strong, protective type. Not afraid to step in and help anyone if he needed to. He was in a lot of fights in high school and was suspended so many times that he was held back a year and had to repeat a grade because of how much he'd missed.

It was something that only attracted me to him more. I guess maybe girls really do fall for the bad boys. Not that he's bad anymore. He's the Captain for Crew A. Keelan is one of his Lieutenants. He's still protective, broody, quiet, and silently strong, but his first instinct now isn't to punch someone out.

Which might be more than I can say for Keelan and Luke. Just as Blake considers me an annoying little sister, Luke is much the same way. And just like Blake and Keelan, Luke is just as protective.

I look up at Keelan. "Don't get in trouble... I just want my stuff."

Keelan kisses the top of my head. "We'll leave your car here. You can ride with me and Luke home. We'll grab his truck and mine and go get your stuff."

I search his eyes. I know my brother. He'll do just that.

But I can't help but notice he didn't say anything about not getting into trouble...

Chapter Two

㊋ Blake ㊋

(One Week Later)

I swirl the warm, hard liquor in my glass and stare down at it. I can already feel the headache starting, but I'm not really sure I care. It's been a damn hard week. Every muscle in my body aches. My brain feels just as fried as a fucking duck egg. As a Captain for our fire department here in Piper Falls, Texas, I have to do a lot more extra training.

Well, maybe I don't have to. But someone has to be able to go to our department heads and fight for new equipment, policies, and procedures for our firefighters. Fuck knows they ain't going to hand it to us on a damn silver platter. We struggle to get the budget we do as it is. Everyone thinks the fire department in every city and town around the world get all they want and need.

I chuckle to myself. If only they knew the shit we need to go through and put up with just to get what we do. And then they get pissed that it takes us nine minutes to respond to calls. Well, give us what we need to get those calls. Maybe then those million dollar homes wouldn't be burnt to the fucking ground before we can show up.

I shake my head and glare into my glass before downing the whiskey. Devil's River. It was brewed in San Antonio, a bit of a drive from here, but it's my favorite. A lot of people probably don't know it's brewed with iron-free limestone spring water. Makes the brew a lot smoother.

Even gives it a little bit of a sweet taste that comes nowhere close to overpowering the spice of it.

Which is everything I need right now.

"Need another, Cap?" Jason Andrews, the twenty-eight year old owner of Papi's asks me.

Papi's Lock 'n' Stock Grill and Bar is one of the most popular of our local bars. It's been a staple of this community for many years. Jason's grandfather built it many years ago from the ground up. His nickname was Papi, so of course, the name of the grill had to reflect that. It serves lunch and dinner, has karaoke every Friday and Saturday nights, and serves the best drinks in Texas.

I might be biased.

The best thing about it, though, is that it's right across the street from the firehall. When we're working our forty-eight hour shifts, it's not hard to grab something to eat from here if we don't want to cook. Or if it's been busy as hell and we don't have the time. Jason and his staff are very good at catering to us and the police department, which is located right next to the firehall.

I nod. "Keep 'em coming."

He chuckles and fills my glass. "Bad day?"

"Bad week." I down the next shot and let it burn going down my throat. "Fuck," I rumble as I set the glass down.

Jason fills it a third time. "Heard you had some training in Colorado."

"Yeah, some forest fire stuff. Had to fight the higher-ups to let me go. I almost paid for the fucking thing out of my own pocket." I take a sip of the whiskey this time and allow myself to savor it as it slides down my throat. A little easier this time, but it still burns.

Jason smiles as he leans down on the counter. He's just over six feet with brown hair. Messy as hell; looks like he just rolled out of bed. His gray eyes light up in a constant smirk. The guy is built like a fucking tank. I don't think anyone would fuck with him. I certainly wouldn't, and I'm four fucking inches taller than he is. I'm muscular in my own right. Still wouldn't want to take him on.

"You know, you're pretty little girl is starting to attract quite the crowd here. She's bringing in a lot of business."

I growl low at him and shoot him a glare as I take another sip of my drink. "Asshole. You know good and fucking well Lila isn't my girl."

"Not like you don't want her to be."

"Would you shut the hell up? I don't need that shit getting around. She's like a little sister to me. Nothing else." Lies. All fucking lies. She's way more than that.

"Mmhmm."

I huff and down the rest of my drink before setting it down. "What the fuck are you doing here anyway? Where's the head bartender? I like her. She's more grandmotherly and not so much of a dick."

Jason stands to his full six foot one inch height and laughs as he switches me to some house brew beer. He sets the glass in front of me. "Ruby is at home with her feet up. Damn woman works more than anyone her age should. You want something to eat to soak up some of this alcohol? Or should I call Luke or Keelan to come get your ass when you're passed out on my bar?"

I can't help but laugh, but he's right. I need to eat something because those drinks are hitting me already. I'd be fine, but I haven't eaten anything all day. "I'll take the nachos."

"Extra jalapenos?"

"Yeah, and throw some hot sauce on there. That shit in the packets don't cut it."

"You got it, Cap."

I nurse my beer as he walks away. I try to keep my mind on anything but the woman he mentioned. Our local celebrity. Talented as hell. Every time she opens her mouth to sing, I swear it's like fucking unicorns and glitter comes out of it. She's mesmerizing. Intoxicating. Spellbinding. One look and she has everyone falling at her feet.

Lila Mancini. She's twenty-two. Seven years my junior. Beautiful beyond my wildest dreams with long, light brown hair and hazel eyes a man could drown in. I have. I have let myself drown in them. Never wanted to come out, but reality is a fucking bitch and fate is fickle.

Lila is my best friend's little sister and way too good for the likes of me.

She's had me under her spell since the moment I met her. And that was when she was just a baby. I've been friends with her brother for most of our lives. Lila was captivating even then. I was in awe of her. As she grew up, I was in awe of her smarts. When she was six, I heard her sing for the first time. She was like my own little sister, only I never thought her annoying like Keelan, her brother, and Luke, our other best friend did. I thought it was cool having her around.

Didn't ever really let her know that, though. I spent my fair share of teasing her.

The older she got, the smarter she got. She became more talented. More beautiful. I don't even know when it was that I started thinking of her as anything more than a sister to me. Maybe it was when she was sixteen and asked me to take her to Homecoming because her boyfriend decided to take some other girl. I was twenty-three then. I almost said yes because fuck anyone who broke that girl's heart, but it would have caused huge problems if she showed up on my arm.

An older guy. One who wasn't even in school anymore. I was a firefighter by then and was working with Keelan and Luke. The Three Musketeers. It's what we'd always been and still are. Inseparable.

I told her no because I didn't want to ruin her reputation or cause issues between me, her, and Keelan. She ended up going with a friend of hers, but called me later that night because her friend left her to go with some senior to "park." We both knew what that meant, and I didn't blame her for not wanting to tag along, even though she had been invited.

So, I picked her up. There was talking and a little more. I'll always be honored to have been her first kiss. To this day, it's our secret. I never told Keelan or Luke, and neither did she, but it was probably that night that changed everything. She'd always preferred to hang out with us guys over her own friends. She never really got along well with other girls. And I didn't mind having her around. She was prettier to look at than my friends, and I enjoyed the way she beat us all at Texas Hold 'Em. How excited she got every single time she won a hand.

She definitely beat them fair and square, but she didn't beat me very many times. Most of the time, I let her win just because of how happy it made her. Nothing in the world, including the Texas sunrise, has ever compared to her smile.

The day of her eighteenth birthday, that all changed. I don't think she has figured it out, but I learned of her feelings for me. More than just that one kiss that made us both run from each other, feelings be fucking damned to the deepest part of Hell. It hit me like a ton of bricks when I saw how she was looking at me. All of those feelings I had for her came rushing back. As soon as she noticed me looking, she quickly turned away.

And I walked away.

I've been keeping as much distance between the two of us as possible. Not to say I'm not still around for her, but I make damn certain she knows it's strictly family. Big brother and little sister type of relationship. No more. Never less. For years, it's torn me up, but it's all it can ever be for us.

And it's worked. For the past few years, I've had a front row seat in watching her talent grow. I've seen her perform in front of huge crowds each year at the County Fair. She has performed at the Fourth of July Day festival out at Jaxon Walker's ranch. She's even performed at huge fairs around the State, including the Texas State Fair. How the assholes in Nashville haven't noticed her is something fuck knows I'll never understand. They don't know what they're missing.

Not that she hasn't tried to get them to take note. She has sent in demos. She has even gone so far as to walk up to a record executive and start crooning to him. The crowd that gathered around her as she sang was one of my proudest moments. Second only to the fact that it was me she asked to bring her there.

But that was over a year ago now, and she still hasn't been signed. She was going to try out for those popular TV talent competitions, but after a lawyer read the type of contract she'd be under if she won, we all decided that it wasn't for her. They'd own her soul, basically. It was something we all would never allow.

I'm so lost in thought, I don't even realize I've absently downed half my nachos and my entire beer. I shake my head to bring myself back to reality, but it doesn't last long. Chills run from the back of my neck and down my spine. My stomach tightens. My fucking cock stirs to life. I don't even need to look to know that Lila is near.

"Hey, man. Glad to see you back," Keelan Mancini says as he sits his muscular six foot frame next to me. He nods to Jason, who promptly grabs him his favorite beer and me a second.

"Glad to be back," I say. And I genuinely am. Even if his sister is way too close to me. I don't know where she is, but I know she's getting closer. I close my eyes to force my reaction to her under control.

"Did you get my message? I thought you'd call back before you went to bed that night."

That worked. My hard dick softens. Instead of my body being tense because of her, it's tense because of the message he left. And the haunting text I got from her that I responded to, but that she never responded back to.

"She sent me a text that just said I was right, and that he's a jerk. But she never responded when I asked her what happened. I meant to call you back, but the training was so fucking grueling, I barely got through a shower before I was asleep. I'm not even sure I ate the entire week."

"Just leave me alone, Daniel!" I look over my shoulder just as Lila, who is sitting in the first booth behind me and the bar, screams. Keelan tenses next to me just before he stands. Lila runs to the bathroom with one of her friends.

I follow Keelan, my protective instincts going into complete overdrive. I don't need to know what's going on. I'm always going to back up my friend; brother, but I'm sure as fuck going to protect her.

Daniel makes a move to follow Lila, but that's never happening. He's not getting near her again. Like an avenging, dark angel, Luke Bradley, in all of his over six feet glory, steps in front of Daniel and shoves him back. Everyone in the bar is looking at us.

The silence is extremely loud and very sobering.

"I thought we made it clear to stay the fuck away from her?" Luke growls as Daniel stumbles.

While the protective instincts over Lila are almost overpowering, the need to protect my best friends, my brothers, from what's about to come if I don't make this shit stop right now is the part of me that's strongest.

As the three friends Daniel is with step up to defend him, I step between Keelan and Luke to defuse the situation. I know damn well we could take them. It's just what comes after that I don't want to deal with.

"Enough," I rumble dominantly. Everyone in this little circle knows who the Alpha male is. There's a reason I'm one of the youngest Captain's our fire department has ever seen. I've held the position for three years. I got it when I was twenty-six. I could probably move even further up the ranks, but I don't want to.

"Walk away, Daniel," Keelen growls dangerously. I know he's on the precipice of throwing a punch.

I glance at Jason. He's not one who will allow this to happen in his bar. I expect him to be striding over here, but I'm shocked to see he's not. He's glaring in our general direction, but he's listening to Lila. I hadn't even seen her come out of the bathroom. She looks like she's holding him back with a hand to his chest, which makes my blood turn green with a jealousy I shouldn't be feeling and have no right to.

I turn back to the scene in front of me. "Back to the bar," I tell Luke and Keelan. "This isn't worth the bullshit that will come from it." I physically push Keelan back when he stands still and keeps glaring.

"Don't come anywhere fucking near her again, you piece of shit," Keelan spits out venomously.

"Not like she's a good lay anyway," one of Daniel's friends says.

"What the hell did you just say?" Keelan barks as he lunges. Keelan may be a big guy, but he's no match for me. Especially when it's me and Luke against him.

"He's not worth it. Blake is right," Luke says, raspily. "We all want to kick his ass, but he's just trying to get a rise out of us. Let it go."

"Get off me," Keelan growls. We both let him go, though slowly. He shakes us off the rest of the way and smooths out his shirt, but it's Lila who calms him the most.

She wraps her arms around him and hugs him. "I have a plan. He and his dirty, STD riddled dick is about to be sorry he met me. I'm about to expose him in the best way I know how."

Her melodic, Southern accented voice gives me those warm and fuzzies, but it's the danger behind those words that has me grinning. Not only do I know she's about to bless us all with a song, but she's also about to put him in his place with her words. Lila has never needed us to protect her. She can handle herself perfectly well.

Before I became a firefighter, maybe even sometime after, I had always resorted to fighting to show my dominance. The Alpha male was constantly getting his hackles raised. Lila, on the other hand, has shown the type of strong, independent woman she is with words. And sometimes, I honestly believe they're more powerful.

She shoots me a smile as she lets go of her brother. She squeezes Luke's arm as she walks back to her table, and that's it for all of us. Just like that, we're all calm. Well, except for my libido, which is fighting its way to the fucking surface once more.

I tear my eyes away from her and sit down at the bar. Luke and Keelan sit on either side of me and order themselves food and drinks. Jason, keeping his eye on Daniel and his asshole friends, puts the order in before grabbing Luke's beer and Keelan's shot. Don't ask what it is. He just asked for something strong.

"So, what the fuck happened while I was gone? Christ. It was just a week, and the entire damn town fell apart." I pop a nacho in my mouth.

"Lila walked in on Daniel screwing some girl on his couch," Luke begins.

I nearly choke as I stare at him. "The fuck?"

"Yep. She was driving home, but ended up stopping at the station because she was crying so hard she couldn't see. Nick saw her and took her to your brother, who called me."

I glare as my head snaps to Keelan while he talks. "I fucking just talked to Elden. He picked me up from the airport. Why the hell would he not tell me that?"

"I don't think he thought it was his place, man," Luke says with a shrug. "None of us did. It's why Keelan only said to give him a call when you can. He was going to have Lila tell you herself."

Keelan pats my back. "Don't worry. He got what's coming to him."

I rub my head. "As much as I hope one of you knocked his ass out and then got another shot in for me, is this something that's going to end with me going up against the higher ups to fight for your jobs?"

Luke laughs. "No. I don't think he's going to say a damn word. He's all tough with his friends to back him up, but Daniel has some secrets. He wouldn't want anyone to know what he did. Lila has a lot more friends and allies than he does, and he knows it. Lila could expose him for the asshole he is, and run him completely out of this town. His business would take a nosedive. He'd never recover from this."

"Then what is she waiting for?" I ask darkly. "Fucking ruin him."

Before anyone has a chance to say a word, music fills the room. We all turn to see Lila taking the stage as soft guitar music plays. The house lights dim. I glance at Keelan and Luke before we all turn in our barstools.

My mouth drops as her usually sweet, very country voice takes on a hard, raspy edge I can honestly say I've never heard before. Her hazel eyes are on fire.

And her glare is leveled on a very uncomfortable and squirming Daniel.

Chapter Three

☉ Lila ☉

"Are you sure you want to do this?" my best friend, Adalle, says. Her pretty blue eyes are filled with concern. She pushes her long blond hair out of her face as she looks at me.

I nod as I take a drink of my fruity Sex on the Beach drink. "Yep." I pop the 'p'.

Faye, my other best friend, bites her lip. "He's powerful enough now to ruin you. He's one of the families who run this town. He's the youngest member of the city council. What if he -?"

I shake my head at her. She huffs out a worried breath before she takes a drink of her strawberry wine cooler. "This needs to be done. And I know my reputation in this town will always be better than his. He started this when he started dropping rumors."

"We don't know if that was him, though," Adalle says, looking down at her whiskey neat.

I shrug. "Who else would it be? And isn't that just like the man he's shown himself to be? This kind, beautiful soul to everyone's face, and pond scum behind closed doors?"

They both just nod, but don't look at me. I'm seething. Since a week ago when I caught him with who I found out was his secretary, Daniel has been doing all he can to get me back. Calling. Texting. Until today, he stayed away from me, probably because of the threat Luke and Keelan made to him when they went to get my stuff. They won't tell me what they said, but it must have worked.

Until now.

Why he picked tonight to approach me when he knew Luke and Keelan were here, I came with them, is beyond me. But it doesn't matter because I've been planning tonight for the entire week. Especially when I walked into my favorite bakery, Bluebonnet Bakery, to get my favorite champagne cupcake and was confronted by Mable, the owner. She told me that she'd heard a few things about me that were so blatantly untrue. I knew it was Daniel that said it.

Things that were meant to hurt me. Like I couldn't get signed to a record label because I tried to sleep with the executives. Or how I have a criminal record a mile long but it's all hidden because I slept with the police. Not just one of them. All of them. Disgusting things like that, but there was one that bothered me the most.

He'd always been jealous of Blake and Luke. So, it shouldn't have been surprising to me when I heard something about me being involved with both of them. With a little of my brother on the side. And it was that rumor that sent me over the edge.

Fuck. Him.

Now, it's my turn. I can't believe how blind and in love I thought I was with him. I can't understand how I felt so giddy and happy around him. Looking back, our entire relationship was him trying to change me. Make me *prettier* by wearing summer dresses and styling my hair. I know my worth. I know I'm already pretty. I don't need to be *prettier* and wear things that make me uncomfortable. I like my jeans, short shorts, and tank tops. I like my flip flops. And if I want to dress up, I do it.

Asshole.

Just thinking of him makes me more and more angry. And with each passing second, I know that what I'm about to do is the right thing. He's not getting away with this. And I'm not going to allow my brother and his friends to fight my battles. Even if they are just as much family to me.

I force thoughts of Blake out of my head with that statement and focus completely on my own little brand of revenge. I take a sip of my drink as the stage is set up by the DJ for tonight's karaoke. People have already signed up, but when I told him what I wanted to do, he grinned and put me ahead of everyone else.

Truthfully, I'm sure that he would have anyway. I'm sort of a local celebrity. I have been since I first performed at our County Fair when I was like twelve or something. It was a talent show that I won. I've always wanted to sing. My mama says I came out singing.

I catch the DJ's eye and he winks as he holds up the microphone for me. I smile as I finish my drink and head towards the stage. My smile grows as I take the mic. My heart beats faster. I turn towards the crowd that's gathered in the bar over the past hour or so since I've been here. The DJ doesn't introduce me. He doesn't have to. Everyone in here knows who I am. Still he usually hypes the singers up, me included.

Not tonight. I asked him not to. I just wanted the music to start. I want Daniel to feel the shock value. I want everyone to be surprised. There aren't many people in this town who don't know he and I were a thing.

I smooth my pink tank top down over my sun-kissed skin. I do the same with my short Daisy Dukes as the music starts. A haunting guitar solo. After a couple of beats, I start singing, my eyes zeroing in on Daniel. Tonight, I will be singing *Red* by Everybody Loves An Outlaw. Perfect for this situation.

> *Did you really think, I'd just forgive and forget, no*
> *After catching you with her*
> *Your blood should run cold, so cold*
> *You, you two-timing, cheap-lying wannabe*
> *You're a fool if you thought that I'd just let this go*

My grip tightens on the mic. My eyes never leave his, but he starts to squirm. It makes me smile just a little as I launch into the chorus, hitting each and every single note just as powerfully as the lead guitar.

> *I see red, red, oh red*
> *A gun to your head, head, to your head*
> *Now all I see is red, red, red*

I sway my hips as I start feeling the music. I'm a power singer, I always have been, but I still have a sweet, country feel. Not tonight. The lights help me to enunciate each word, giving it more of a live show feeling than a karaoke session.

Did you really just say, she didn't mean anything, oh
I'll remember those words when I come for your soul, your soul
Know that you, you dug your own grave, now lie in it
You're so cruel, but revenge is a dish best served cold

All eyes are now flicking between me and Daniel as people start putting two and two together. Daniel is sinking down further into his seat while his friends glare at me. While I'm thoroughly enjoying it all, there's only one pair of eyes I care about.

And I can feel them on me. He gives me the bravery and strength I need to keep going. So, I launch into the next part with all I am as I lose myself in the words.

I see red, red, oh red
A gun to your head, head, to your head, oh
Executioner style, and there won't be no trial
Don't you know that you're better off dead?
All I see is red, red, oh red
Now all I see is

I let my eyes fall closed as the smile on my lips grows into more of a smirk. I lose myself in the lead guitar solo for a few beats until it leads me back into the words of the song. Once again, I open my eyes.

Run, hide
Oh, you're so done
Oh, better sleep with one eye open tonight

The music steadily gets faster, and I feel it in my soul. I throw all of my emotions into each and every single word, making sure to punctuate them each with all of the anger I feel. Daniel isn't even looking at me anymore. His friends are still glaring at me. Everyone else is cheering and whistling.

And Blake's voice rises above them all.

I see red, red, oh red, oh

24

A gun to your head, head, to your head, oh
Executioner style, and there won't be no trial
Don't you know that you're better off dead?
All I see is red, red, oh red
Now all I see is red, red

As the music leads me out, the light guy the DJ hires does something with the lights that makes me feel like I'm on a real stage. Red lights flash like a strobe light as the music fades out. It gives me such an adrenaline rush and makes the crowd go wild. I'll never get tired of this feeling.

I give the mic back to the DJ with a smile. "Ladies and gentlemen," he begins. "Give it up for our own Lila Rose!"

He says nothing more, but everyone in the bar whoops, hollers, and claps. There's whistling. As I step off the stage, people congratulate me and tell me what a jerk Daniel is. How they'll never use the company of a dirty asshole like him. One of the guys standing next to his girlfriend tells me he's canceling his contract.

I wish I could say I feel bad, but while Daniel escapes the daggers and dirty looks being thrown at him as he and his friends leave the bar, I don't feel an ounce of pity. Everything that's coming to him is so beyond well-deserved.

Adalle and Faye both hug me and giddily tell me that it worked out better than they thought it would. People were whispering about the rumors about me and seemed disgusted that Daniel would stoop so low when he's the one who wronged me.

"We're going to get going, Lils," Faye says after a few moments.

"Awe." I pout. "The night is just getting started."

Adalle laughs. "I, unfortunately, have to adult tomorrow. I took an overtime shift at the hospital. One of the registrars needed a break. We've been splitting her shifts all week. Tomorrow is mine."

"And I have an early flight to New York."

I smile and nod. "I understand." I hug them both again. "Good luck with your audition, girl." I kiss her cheek. "Break a leg!"

She giggles. "I've been waiting forever for this."

"We're so excited for you," Adalle says with a huge grin. "Our friend from small-town Piper Falls going out there and taking on New

York. We can't wait to see your name up in bright lights on the marquee sign."

Faye squeaks and blushes before turning to me. "And you. Your name is going to be in neon lights all over the world soon."

I blush and push them both lightly towards the door. "Go, y'all. You have busy days ahead. I want to hear everything."

They both hug me again and head out. I watch them both leave before letting out the breath I'd been holding. I don't want anyone to know how close I am to falling apart. I might be comfortable in front of people singing, but I realize what I just did. I may not feel bad for what will happen to him, but I'm not immune to the fact that I'm the cause of the fallout. The retaliation I'm sure someone like him will rain down on me is scary to think about.

I hug myself and head for the bar. I need a water or something. Anything to ease my racing heart and upset stomach.

I need Blake.

Something I'll never tell him, but just being near him is enough for me. He calms me like no other. He always has. Even when I was just a little kid, there was always something about him. Keelan and Luke always teased him about it. How I loved him better than them. They all laughed it off, and as family, I don't love either of them more than the other.

It's just that there has always been something about Blake that's eased me. He's my safe harbor in the rough seas. His spicy ocean scent has always been what I've needed to relax when I don't think I can. His commandingly powerful voice that always takes on a sweeter tone with me...

I keep my eyes lowered until I'm able to get my emotions back in check. I should have known that wouldn't work. Not around these three guys. They know me better than anyone.

I step between Blake's legs as he wraps his arms around me. "That was one fuck of a form of revenge. I don't think his company will survive until sunrise."

"I don't think he'll survive until sunrise. I think a lot of the guys in here who are in love with you are planning to go out with pitchforks and torches." Luke grins at me as I sniffle and look at him over Blake's shoulder.

"He deserves it," Keelan rumbles as he rubs my back.

Blake pushes me back slightly and settles me so I'm sitting on his lap. There's not a single stool open. I'm sure he knows Luke or Keelan would give them up for me, but he knows me well. This is what I need. I might not ever get more, but at least I get him close.

"You don't seem too happy about that," he says as he nods at Jason.

"Oh, I -"

"She'll take a water," Blake says when Jason is within ear shot.

I blink a few times. "How do you do that?" I ask quietly.

He shrugs. "I know you."

Jason sets water in front of me, and I take a few sips of the cold liquid. After a few moments, I finally open up. It's not like I'd be able to keep it from any of them anyway. "I'm afraid he's going to retaliate. He's already started rumors."

"Bullshit rumors, Lils," Keelan says. "Everyone knows you're not involved with Luke and Blake. And they certainly all know that I'm not sitting there watching and joining in."

I open my mouth to say something, anything, as my heart stops beating and my eyes fly to Blake for his reaction. He's been training this last week and just got back today. He has no idea the things that have been going on. I haven't been able to tell him. I wanted to, but it seemed so impersonal to tell him in a text or on the phone.

Blake's face reveals nothing but anger, though. And I know it's not directed at me. I glance at Luke and Keelan because I can't speak, but I don't know why Blake isn't throwing things or yelling at that tidbit of information. He hates things dropped on him like that, but what's more is that he's super protective of all three of us and those he's close to. I've seen him come to blows with people over us before.

"We told him while you were up there, Lils," Luke explains.

Keelan chuckles. "Seemed like the best time while we were all listening to you take Daniel down a peg or two."

"I'm pissed, Lila, but I don't think I need to do a damn thing. You did just fine on your own." Blake squeezes my thigh.

I inhale sharply and glance at Keelan instantly thankful he didn't notice. Keelan has no idea how I feel about Blake. He doesn't know that we have a little bit of history. He doesn't know that Blake was my first kiss. He has no clue that we've been on a very up and down ride for years that spans between flirting to strictly something platonic. He doesn't know that being near Blake makes everything in me settle.

He doesn't know I've been so in love with Blake for so long. No one does. It's been something I've kept locked up tight. I certainly haven't told Keelan. I'm not sure what he'd do with that information, but I wouldn't put it past him to try to kill Blake. Maybe not actually kill him, but I don't doubt it would put a wedge between them. Keelan loves Blake like a brother, but not even Blake is good enough for me in his eyes. And I don't want to be the cause of any quarrels between them.

Luke, on the other hand, is very neutral. I doubt he'd say a word if I opened up to him. Hell, he's observant enough. He probably knows. He seems to always just know things. It's part of his charm. At least that's what I always tell him. It's honestly unnerving.

I push everything out of my mind, though, as I sit securely on Blake's lap. It's not something I've never done before. In fact, it's so normal that no one ever bats an eye at it.

Which is why I allow Blake to do what he does best.

Relax me.

Though this is all it will ever be for us, even if my traitorous heart keeps a spark of hope that one day that will change, it's something that keeps me warm at night.

And calms the tumultuous hurricane in my heart.

Chapter Four

☯ Blake ☯

(Three Weeks Later)

"You'll be okay, Mrs. Peterson," I say as our paramedics load the eighty-year-old woman into the back of the ambulance.

"Thanks to you, young man. Thanks to you," she whispers with tears in her eyes.

I smile. "Take care, darlin.'" I close the doors and tap them so the driver knows his partner and patient are safely secured inside.

"Nice save, Cap," Ashe Embers, one of my younger guys on my crew says when I turn back around. "I never would have guessed she was choking. She was talking."

"Sometimes, things ain't as they appear," I tell him with a tired smile as I look at my watch.

It's been a long day, and I'm fucking tired. Who am I kidding? This whole fucking shift has been straight from hell. I need a damn break. I scrub my hands down my face as I jump in the passenger seat of our ladder truck. I close my eyes and lean my head back on the headrest.

"Doing okay?" Luke asks me from the driver seat after everyone is settled and he starts driving.

I don't open my eyes. "Yeah. We need to do some grocery shopping. Stop at the store on the way back."

"You got it."

"What are the chances we can get you to make a cheesecake for dessert tonight?" Ashe asks.

I grin. "Depends. Who has the Excedrin to get rid of this fucking headache?"

"There's some in my locker," Keelan rumbles. "Replenished my stock after last shift."

"Motherfucker, last shift sucked a donkey's ass," James Skarin, my second Lieutenant says.

"Man, I agree completely. I almost said fuck firefighting after that shit," Keelan agrees.

I grin. "Literally. Shit."

Everyone laughs. Our last shift involved a geyser of sewer shit. After it was all dealt with and contained, we each spent a good hour in the shower. Had any fires happened or any other calls came in, we might have ignored everything just so we could feel clean again. And that wasn't even the end.

I put my elbow on the window frame and rest my head on my hand. Last shift wasn't one I'd ever want to repeat. After the geyser of shit call, we got a call from a kid saying his daddy was in trouble in the bathroom. When we arrived, the four-year-old was sitting on the porch with his knees drawn up to his chest. He looked like he'd been crying, but what struck me is that the tears had dried. He wasn't crying anymore. Just waiting patiently for us as he was talking to our dispatcher. He led us to his dad like a very brave little boy.

No one expected what we walked into. In the bathroom was a naked man puking in the toilet. He was very obviously in distress, but that's not what had any of us the most concerned. It was the handle of the plunger sticking out of his ass.

There were a lot of questions. Way more thoughts about how it happened. But we all jumped into action quickly because our concern went from the plunger to the amount of blood he was throwing up. We quickly got him loaded into an ambulance and sent him and his son to the hospital, but before our paramedics arrived, we got the story.

He'd taken a shower, slipped on his way out, and landed perfectly on the plunger. Considering the destruction of the bathroom, the story was far more plausible than some of the thoughts we had going through our minds.

Ashe did pretty good until the very end when he threw up in a bush. The rest of us waited until after we'd gotten back to the station before we all lost the contents of our own stomachs. After cleaning up again, I called to see how he was. I don't know how they did it, considering the blood coming out of him, but they saved his life. Turns out, it went so deep, he had internal bleeding and damage, but they believed he'd, miraculously, make a full recovery.

It was a pretty good ending to the complete shit of a day we'd had.

A couple of hours later, I have a cheesecake in the oven as I make burgers for dinner. The guys are settling. Considering how busy we've been, them settling makes me believe we're going to get a call at any second.

I start flipping the burgers, and it's at that moment that my phone rings. I glance at the number before I answer it. I'm surprised to see the name that flashes across my screen. "Captain Falcon," I rumble as I hold it between my ear and shoulder while I cook.

"Blake! It's James Maxton with Destiny Records."

"Yeah, hey! It's nice to hear from you."

"Just wanted to check in and let you know I didn't forget about you or your girl. I'm in talks with some partners about her, but can you shoot us a demo?"

I start plating things and swallow hard. I've been good at keeping Lila out of my mind most of the day, but she's back full fucking force now. "Shit. Uh. I think she did send a demo. I know she sent them to a lot of record companies."

"Just no offers."

"Not only that. Blatant rejection. Even with a face to face audition that drew a lot of people off the streets."

"I showed my partners the short video clip you sent, and they're interested. I'll do some digging. See if we have a demo from her. Lila Rose, right?"

"Yes, sir. I'll get you a demo, too. Just in case."

"I'll text you the address to get it directly to my desk."

"Perfect. Thank you."

"You're welcome. Things are looking good."

I grin. "Damn, I'm glad to hear that. Appreciate it. It's been a long time coming."

"Glad it was you they sat me next to on that plane ride!"

I laugh as we say our goodbyes. After I have everything set out, I whistle for the boys. They all know it means the food is done and to get their asses to the table to eat. It only takes seconds for everyone to be gathered at the table and seated.

I sit at the head of the table. I don't know when it all happened, but it was decided long before my time that the Captain always sits at the head of the table. It's like he's the father of the crew. I suppose that would be true for most departments, but we have a lot of younger Captains here. Our whole department is mostly filled with young guys and girls.

Everyone falls into easy conversation and feeds Murphey, our firehouse dog, table scraps. I chip in where I need to and chuckle at how spoiled my dog is. I adopted him as a puppy. I found him abandoned. No one ever came forward to claim him. He grew on me, so I officially adopted him, but he became everyone's dog. Whenever I go for training, Luke takes him for me. He might love Murphey more than even I do, but it's fine with me because I know he's well taken care of when I'm not around.

Murphey is four years old now and even comes with us on calls. He's not officially trained or anything, but he has helped out a good number of times. One particular time was when we were helping the police look for a missing kid who got away from his parents. I still maintain to this day that we wouldn't have found him if Murphey hadn't been there. He sniffed him out so easily, it was almost comical. The kid, who is now six, still comes to see Murphey and thank him for helping him. Damn dog is cockier than I am, so he loves the attention everyone gives him.

After dinner as the guys are cleaning up, I take the opportunity to lay down. My headache hasn't gone away. Thank God for blackout shades. The bedroom for us firefighters takes up half of the top floor. There's a bed for each firefighter, eighteen in total on all of our units. Murphey jumps up on my bed with me and lays his head on my stomach.

I chuckle and look down at him. "You know this bed is barely big enough for me. Have you seen me?" I run my fingers through his fur and scratch behind his ears. He licks his chops and closes his eyes, nuzzling into my six pack abs. "You're an asshole."

"Talking to animals now?" Keelan asks with a grin.

I drop an arm over my eyes and groan. "Fifteen minutes. That's all

I need. Cover for me."

He chuckles. I hear him sit on the bed next to mine. "Not here for anything work related."

"Then shoot."

"I'm going to be a little late getting to the Fourth Fest at Walker Estate. Lila needs to get there a little early for sound check. She doesn't want to drive. She wants to have a little fun this time. I promised I'd pick Faye up from the airport. She's been back and forth between here and New York since she got hired with the theater company. And Adalle is working until later on."

I can't get away from her even if I try. I've been good about avoiding her since the night she took down her ex at Papi's. Since I made the colossal mistake of having her in my lap. And the even more epic mistake of rubbing her hip or squeezing her thigh. She probably took it as comfort, but it was me being fucking selfish and letting myself think that, for a few seconds, she was mine. Just long enough to get me through for a little while.

"Why can't Luke grab her?" I ask, a little more gravelly than I intended.

Keelan is quiet for so long, I almost fall asleep. When he finally speaks, I jump. "Did something happen to make you not want to? You've been acting weird since that night at Papi's."

Leave it to Keelan to pick up on that shit. I sigh but stay still. "It's nothing like that. I just wasn't sure I was going to go this year. I'm fucking exhausted. I can see the fireworks from my porch. I was thinking a quiet night in with Murphey and a beer."

"Dude. Come on. What's going on? You love the Fourth Fest."

If only I could tell you. It's not like I *like* keeping things from him. I've been through hell with Keelan and Luke. The only reason Jason knows how I feel about Lila is because the motherfucker caught me watching her one night, and I spilled my drunken guts to him before going home with a random hose ho, a girl who loves sleeping with a firefighter. No matter if he's married, engaged, seeing someone or not. She just wants him because she likes the fact that he's a firefighter.

"Nothing, Keelan. Really. I'm fine. I'm just fucking tired. This headache is killing me. I forgot tomorrow was the Fourth. I was looking forward to a night of recovery."

He's quiet again for a few moments. "Okay," he says finally. "I'll ask Luke."

I sigh again. "No. I got her, Keelan. You're right. I'd be pissed off at myself for not going."

He pats my thigh as he stands. "Good."

"Hey, before you go. Don't tell Lila this. I don't want her hopes up just in case it doesn't work out, but I met someone from Destiny Records on the plane on the way back from Colorado. We got to talking. I showed him a clip of Lila singing and sent it to him. He called today and said he's been talking about her to his partners. It looks promising, but they'd like a demo."

"She sent them one. She sent one to every label in Texas, Nashville, Cali, and the Big Apple."

"Well, given what he said, I suspect that a lot of them are screened. He texted me his home address. He said he was going to text an address to make sure it got directly to him. I didn't think it would be his house, but I'll take it." I crack an eye open.

Keelan is grinning. "Hell yeah. I'll get you a demo. And I won't lead her on by telling her anything."

I smile and close my eye again. "Good. Now, get the fuck out. I need to get rid of this damn thing. Tell everyone to get some sleep while they can."

"You got it, Cap."

What seems like seconds later, with my arm draped across my eyes and my fingers buried in Murphey's fur, I'm passed the fuck out.

Chapter Five

✹ Lila ✹

I hum as I finish putting my hair up. I take the clip I'm holding in my mouth and slide it in my hair to hold it all in place. I finish my look off with a yellow hairband that matches my sunflower yellow dress. I smile and spin around in front of my mirror.

"Perfect." I smooth down my dress. It hits mid-thigh, and I'm a big fan of how it fans out at my hips. It's light and flowy. Paired with my black, leather cowboy boots, I'm definitely stage ready. I love how the dress against my skin makes my skin look darker and brightens my eyes.

He has always liked my eyes; said I look pretty in yellow.

I sigh at myself and close my eyes. I can't do this again. I refuse to allow myself to go through what I do with Blake. I know he doesn't pine for me. I lost count of the number of women I've seen him go home with. Every time it happens, it breaks me a little more.

It's not fair.

I don't even have to talk to him about any of this to know his reasoning for not wanting me. I even understand. It's not his fault I've got some stupid crush on my brother's best friend. How cliche of me. Maybe I should write a song about it.

Ha! Not like I haven't already. Every song I've ever written has been about Blake Falcon. And the longer I'm away from Daniel, the more I realize seeing him screwing his secretary was for the best. It saved us both. He doesn't have to be tied down to the likes of me, someone obviously not good enough for him, and I don't have to be stuck with him, someone who will never measure up to the firefighter who has my heart.

I'll never have him, though. Guess I'm just destined to be alone because no one will measure up to him. I compare everyone to him. Anyone I am ever with or have ever been with is nothing more than a settlement. They'll never be Blake.

Crazy.

Insane.

I should be in a psych ward. My mind is so jumbled, I can't even form a coherent thought. Classic psycho.

I let out a breath when I hear a vehicle pulling up in front of the house. My heart knows it's Blake. I know the sound of his brand-new, shiny red, Ford F-150 SCA Performance truck anywhere. He went all out with the Black Widow features and Raptor tires. He even has a six-inch lift on it and automatic running bars. He pushes a button or something, and down they come. His windows are tinted. The interior is all black leather. Blake spared no expense.

I take a big, deep breath before opening the door. Blake is almost to it and wearing his trademark grin. Slightly cocky. A whole lotta sexy. I hate everything about the way he looks so mouthwatering in his tight jeans and plain red t-shirt. Even his messy hair looks stupidly handsome. He's breathtaking and doesn't even try.

"You look beautiful, Miss America. Ready to go?" His grin widens.

I involuntarily shiver as I nod. He's the only one who calls me Miss America. "Yeah." I turn to shut the door and attempt to get myself in check.

As I turn back to Blake, his large hand finds the middle of my back and slides down to just above my butt. I can feel his heat even through the fabric of my dress, and it makes me hate him even more.

Except I don't hate him. Not at all.

I hate myself for loving him as I do.

I let out a breath as he opens the passenger side door for me. I give him a soft smile as he helps me into the truck. I melt into the cool, soft leather. He'd kept the truck running and air going for the few seconds it took me to get out here. It's so hot, and he's so thoughtful. One more thing on the Grand Canyon sized list of things that makes me love him as I do.

36

There's no chance for recovery for me. Not unless I leave town. It's the only option at this point. I love Piper Falls and everyone in it, but Blake makes me want to run. Anything to clear my head and heart from the suffocation of him.

Blake reaches up for my seatbelt and pulls it across me. I jump and stare at him as he clicks it into place. He raises an eyebrow in concern. "You okay?"

"Y-yeah." I shake my head and close my eyes for a moment before opening them. "Yeah." I give him another soft smile, but I know I'm blushing. His hand is sending goosebumps all over my skin.

He squeezes my thigh and gives me that stupid, hot smile again. "Okay." He closes my door, and I sink into the soft leather of the seat as I hug myself. Seconds later, he's jumping in the truck.

I clear my throat, needing any kind of a distraction from how amazing he looks in his distressed jeans. They're my favorite of his. I know he knows that, but I don't want to read into it. I know where we stand. I always have.

"Thank you for taking me. Keelan said you didn't want to go." I keep my eyes straight ahead, refusing to look up at him.

"Just tired. I planned on drinking a beer and sitting on my porch to watch the fireworks with Murphey."

I nod and look outside the passenger side window instead. Anything to keep him out of my vision completely so I don't cry. I take a breath. "You never miss the Festival," I almost whisper.

He's quiet for a few moments as he drives. I hear him take a breath before his hand is on my thigh. "Lila, look at me." He squeezes my thigh, but I don't look at him. Instead, I blink away the tears and shake my head. "Lila. I said look at me." His deep, Southern accented voice drops an octave and sounds far deeper. So dominant that I can't stop myself from obeying him.

I look at him, but my eyes drop again, this time to his hand on my thigh. My very bare thigh. "It's fine, Blake."

"Talk to me, honey. What's wrong?" His thumb lightly strokes my thigh. "Is it Daniel? Because if he's there -"

I shake my head. "No. No, it's nothing to do with him. I just don't want to talk about it."

He falls silent as he removes his hand from my thigh while he makes the turn down the long road that leads to Walker Estate. "I kinda get the feeling you're upset with me," he says after a few moments.

I can't help but chuckle. "We haven't talked hardly at all the past few weeks. I know you had that training, but you've been avoiding me. I know you have been. What I don't know is why." I look up at him finally. "Did I do something -"

He shakes his head. "No. Lila, no. It's nothing you did. It's me. I've been fucked up over the past three weeks. The training was hard on me. I haven't recovered. I'm sore. I've barely even worked out the last three weeks because I've been so damn exhausted." He glances at me as he rests his elbow on the center console. He opens his hand as he looks back at the road. "I promise my hiding away has nothing at all to do with you. Friends still?"

I look at his hand as the tightening in my chest begins to unfurl. Finally, I put my small hand in his much larger one. "Always." Because that's all we'll ever be. It's all we can be. No matter how much I want it to be different, it never will be.

Blake squeezes my hand as he pulls into Walker Estate. Jaxon Walker waves as Blake lets go of my hand. I instantly miss the warmth of it, but as we get out, I'm blasted with dry, Texas air. Blake meets me at my door and helps me down from his truck. I love how he towers over me. This truck is perfect for him. Too big for me, but he needs it to be. He's so big himself.

He opens the back door and reaches in for something. When he pops back out with a worn out, brown cowboy hat on his head, I can't help but crack up. He grins and gives me a matching one that only makes me laugh harder.

"How have you kept these so long?" I ask after I finally calm down.

His grin grows as he leans in to whisper in my ear. "You think I'm going to get rid of the hat you were wearing when I kissed you? Fuck no."

My eyes snap to his. "I... thought..." My heart starts racing. I can't speak. I can't even think.

He raises an eyebrow. "You think I got rid of it?"

Is he closer? He feels closer. He looks closer.

Is it hot because of the heat? Or am I sweating because of him?

One of my hands flies to my chest in an effort to keep my

pounding heart inside my body where it belongs. "I l-left it in your truck that night... I never saw it again."

"Well." He puts the smaller hat that matches his on top of my head, being careful with my hair. It's up, but not all the way. Some of it is still cascading down my back. I was regretting not putting it all up, but that feeling is long gone. "Maybe I just didn't want to give it back."

His lips are so close to mine. I close my eyes because I'm convinced our lips are about to meet. I already feel my body exploding into a thousand fireworks brighter than the ones I'm sure we'll see tonight.

"Lila! We're all ready for you!" Jaxon calls.

My eyes fly open. Blake takes several steps back from me as if whatever spell he was under had been abruptly broken. He clears his throat. I watch the cocky asshole facade he carries everywhere with him slip into place. Seconds later, he's leading me to the stage like nothing at all happened.

Holy shit.

Did I dream that?

After what I feel like is forever, the sound is finally where it needs to be. I won't actually be performing until a little later, the music is mostly being done by a DJ, but I perform our National Anthem and a few other songs that are patriotic every single year. It's something I love doing so much.

Throughout the day, Blake is good about making sure I'm hydrated. He's constantly bringing me water and being so attentive to me. He made sure I got a break, since it's so hot. He even made me take a time out when I started sweating. He stayed near the stage the entire time and watched me with this proud look on his face.

It's nothing that Blake hasn't done before. The issue is that he is doing this right after I swore he was going to kiss me by his truck. I feel like I'm still in a daze from that; from the fact that he kept a hat I thought I'd lost so many years ago. He *kept* it and didn't tell me he had it. Which means he kept it intentionally.

What does that even mean?

"You looked great up there," he says to me as I step down the stairs. He takes my hand, guiding me the rest of the way. "Doing okay? Want to go sit in the shade for a little while? Keelan just showed up with Faye."

"Faye! I can't believe she got time off to come home for the weekend." For a brief moment, I forget about everything but my friend and how happy I am that she's here.

And then he does it.

He pulls me close and hugs me.

It's so hot out here, but he still smells strong and oaky. A masculine scent mixed with him. Nothing will ever come close to it. Usually I'd be pushing people away in weather like this. Who in their right mind wants to be hugged by someone in temps like these? Sweat slicked bodies getting even more damp.

But oh God… I want to stay here. Right here in his arms. It feels so right. It has always felt so right. Like I belong with him and only him.

Way, way too soon, and he's letting go. I almost whimper at the loss, but I know it doesn't mean as much to him as it does to me. He's not the crazy one who is totally in love with someone who is untouchable.

"You really were great up there. My own Miss America."

I smile and blush then swat him. "I'm not Miss America."

He shrugs. "Debatable." He grins and leads me out to Keelan and Faye.

"Lily Pad!" Faye shouts when she sees me behind Blake. Lily Pad. I don't know where she got that, but she's the only one who calls me it. She once said it was because I was so pretty, like the most beautiful lily Pad. Wisely, Blake steps out of the way as Faye runs to me. We hug each other hard as we jump up and down, squealing.

"I missed you so much! How is New York? How is the production? You got hired so fast! I have so many questions!"

"Oh gosh, it's so fun! It's everything I dreamed. And everyone is really so nice. It's like a family." She tugs me down with her as she sits. I don't notice that she sat me next to Blake until it's too late. His scent fills my entire being.

And when I lean against him as I settle on the bench, he doesn't pull away. Just keeps talking to Keelan and Luke about something. I don't know what they're talking about because my senses are overloaded with Blake. I barely hear Faye talk. It angers me because I was so excited about what she had to say, but Blake has managed to make me miss half of the words leaving her mouth.

And he hasn't even done a damn thing.

I shiver when I feel his fingers on my lower back. "Want some food, Lily?" Blake rumbles close to my ear. Heat pools at my core at his shortened version of Faye's nickname for me.

"Sure," I say softly with an unsure smile. He smiles, setting me at ease somehow.

By the time the sun is just beginning to dip below the horizon, Blake has me so confused. He escorts me to the stage, and I finally turn to him bravely.

"What's happening right now?" I ask.

He raises an eyebrow. "What do you mean?" He tucks a strand of hair behind my ear.

"This, Blake," I say softly. "I… thought…" I trail off and take a breath. "It's just that I've always known where we've stood, but this… It's starting to feel like…" I can do nothing more but look up at him and search his beautiful eyes.

I can see the exact moment it all dawns on him as he nods slowly. "I'm sorry. I let my guard down and led you on. I didn't mean to, Lila. Nothing has changed. It can't."

I swallow hard as I nod and turn. I make my way onto the stage when the DJ announces me. I take my microphone and force myself into performance mode.

Lila Rose is tough. Fearless. Nothing gets to her.

Nothing.

I won't let him see my broken heart. The one only he's managed to shatter into so many pieces that it gets so much harder to put back together each time. Not even Daniel broke me like this. What he did never hurt me as much as Blake.

Blake won't see me cry.

No one will.

Chapter Six

☽ Blake ☾

The fireworks display is gorgeous, as always. Jaxon Walker always puts on the best show. It's probably why this festival is one of the most popular in the area. Good thing the guy has plenty of room and is able to afford to accommodate everyone who comes. Though, I know that many in the area help him out. Some probably even donate their time, among other things. Tables, chairs, benches, food, music, the stage.

My eyes aren't on the display, though. My mind isn't even on the festival at all. All of my attention is focused on the woman on stage. The beautiful woman who I spent all fucking day leading on. The one I almost lost myself to and kissed.

The same girl I just pushed away and hurt all over again. Something I vowed I'd never do again. Not after I saw how our kiss so many years ago built her up only for me and my decision to keep my distance afterwards destroyed her.

Now, as she stumbles over the words to *America The Beautiful*, it's happening all over again. She just went through a lot with her ex, flourished and rose above, only to be burned to ashes once more by me. Someone who is supposed to be there for her.

She tries to keep her eyes off me, but as she fights to get through the words, her gaze keeps finding mine. What I see in her usually bright eyes tears me apart little by little. It's so obvious that the feelings she has for me that I saw so long ago have never died. The older I get, the harder it is for me to fight what I feel for her.

But I know that I have to. As much as it's going to kill both of us, I know exactly what I need to do. She has to be over me for good. She doesn't deserve what's about to happen any more than she deserves to be hung up on someone she can never be with. Not only am I not good enough for her, but us being together would break my relationship with her brother.

While I don't want that, I could take it a lot better than she'd be able to. The tension that would inevitably happen between me and Keelan would destroy her little by little. I'll never allow that. I'd never let something come between her and those she loves the most. That's how much I love her. Enough to let her go for good.

And that's what's about to happen. I'm going to lose her forever. I don't want to hurt her, but she'll be okay. She has a lot of people to get her through it. My punishment will be suffering in silence because no one can know just how much I want her.

She deserves to live her life to the fullest and love someone who will love her back with just as much passion. Not the drama I'd bring into her life. She's got so much going for her. Her name is going to be in bright lights. I can't compare to all she's worth.

When Lila messes up once more, I can see she's about to cry. So, I get up and head towards one of the tents near the stage. It's the one Lila will have to go through when she's done. On my way, though, I seek out one of the girls in the crowd who I know will be willing to help me with my plan. Someone who doesn't give a shit about anything more than the uniform I put on; the badge I pin to my chest.

I stop by the giant cooler and grab a beer. I've lost count of how many I've had, but I've secured a ride home, at least. Thank fuck for my brother and Luke, who plans to drive my truck home for me. Just as I'm downing the rest of my beer, Luke appears at my side.

"You sure about this?" he asks. Luke is the only one who knows about my feelings for Lila and my plan. And it's only because he pulled me aside and asked me what the fuck was going on. I never drink as much as I am right now. I should quit. I'm damn near alcohol poisoning level.

"Nope." I drop my bottle in the garbage. "But it's the only option."

"Why not just tell her?"

I sigh as I look at him. He still looks too clear for my liking. Not blurred enough. And there's still only one of him. "I told you why." I reach for another bottle, but stumble.

Luke catches me. "Yeah. You did, but I still think you're being stupid."

"I'm not putting a wedge between me and Keelan or her and Keelan." I attempt to go for another beer again.

"Blake. Enough." He tugs me away from the cooler. "No more. You're gonna be so drunk by the time you leave tonight, you're not going to even make it to the truck. You know I'm ride or die with you, but this plan is the stupidest thing you've ever come up with. And that includes throwing paint balloons at the principal's house junior year."

"It has to be done. It's the only way."

"It's not the only way. You're being stubborn. I don't support this. At all. You know Keelan is suspicious as fuck right now."

I flinch a little. Luke doesn't usually swear unless he's pissed off. "Well, as long as it saves relationships, it'll be fine."

Luke glares. "Saves relationships except yours, right?"

"That's what I'm trying to do, Luke!"

His glare darkens. "I meant with her," he hisses.

I shake my head and take a step back to steady myself because I'm suddenly dizzy from the movement. "I'm doing it. End of story."

"For fuck's sake," he rumbles. "I'm taking your truck to your house. I'll meet Elden there. I'm not going to stick around for the show."

I breathe a sigh of relief as Luke turns on his heel and heads for my truck. I scrub my hands down my face. Lila is just starting the National Anthem. She can't see me from where I am and hasn't messed up the lyrics since I disappeared from her view. I'm taking it as a sign. She's way better off without me.

I scan the crowd quickly, avoiding Keelan and the table I was at completely. When my eyes find the girl I know will help me out tonight, I make a beeline for her. Charlotte. A few years ago, we had a brief fling. She's definitely a hose ho, but she's a little more to me. After we broke up, we stayed friends. She's helped me out of more sticky situations with women than I care to admit. I've done the same for her.

When I reach her, I put my hands on her shoulders and squeeze just a little as I lean down. "I need your help," I whisper in her ear.

She looks back at me with a wide smile that shows way too much of her mouth. "Why Blake Falcon," she drawls. "What can I do for you, sweetheart?"

I grin and hold out my hand as I glance at the stage. "Just come with me. I'll explain."

She takes my hand, and I pull her with me to the tent Lila will be entering in just a few minutes from now. "What's the hurry, sugar?" she asks me when I get her where I need her to be. Sugar. Fuck, that makes me want to puke.

"I need to make Lila pissed at me. Enough that she never wants to speak to me or be near me again."

She furrows her brows and folds her arms over her chest. "Okay, why?"

"Because she deserves better than me."

She shakes her head, confused. "Are you drunk?"

I grin. "Yeah. Definitely. But that's not the point. This needs to happen."

She glances over her shoulder as the music comes to an end and the grand finale of the fireworks begins. She looks back at me. "What's going on?"

"It's a long story, Charlotte. To make it short, she has feelings for me. I have them for her. But she's way better than I am and deserves more than I could ever give her. And then there's Keelan. I don't want to ruin our relationship. Me with her would drive a wedge between us. You know how protective he is of her. No one is good enough for her. That wedge between us would tear Lila apart. I'm not going to do that either. Best thing to do is make her pissed the fuck off at me so she'll be forced to forget about her feelings for me."

She shakes her head again. "And what about you, Blake?"

I shrug. "What about me?"

"This is going to hurt you."

"I can take it. This happens. Everything goes on the same as it was."

"Minus her in your life, Blake. This is not a smart idea. You know I'll help you with anything you ask…"

"Then help me with this."

She sighs and glances over her shoulder again. Her shoulder-length blond hair brushes her skin. She hugs herself even tighter, pushing up her large tits. The white tank top she's wearing over her tight jean skirt leaves nothing about her to the imagination. The girl is beautiful. She's slender with great muscle tone, but she's not my type.

Finally, she looks back at me. "Okay, but this is a terrible idea, Blake. You're gonna destroy that lil' girl."

"She has support, Char. And she won't tell anyone this has to do with me." I don't tell her why. She doesn't have to know. I rub my head as I sway a little.

I feel Charlotte's hands on my stomach. "Fine. But here she comes, so you better do what you're going to do and fast."

I waste no time. I pull her close and wrap my arms around her. I lean down and kiss her long and hard, swiping my tongue over hers and sucking lightly. She inadvertently whimpers into my mouth and moans just like I want her to. Her arms wrap around me. Her hands find my ass and squeeze. I look over her, my lips still locked to hers and see Lila just getting to the stairs. Her head is down. She hasn't seen us yet.

I take the opportunity to push Charlotte's skirt up enough to grip her ass underneath the fabric. She's not wearing underwear, I didn't expect she would be, and I have to keep my eyes on Lila in order to get myself through this.

I plunge my tongue deeper into Charlotte's mouth like I'm fucking her with it and pull her even more snuggly to my body. She whimpers once more, making Lila look up, startled. When she sees me, her eyes widen. I keep kissing Charlotte. I lower my eyes so Lila can't see me watching her, even though I still am.

I hear her gasp just before her pretty hand covers her mouth. She stares at us in disbelief before tears start to fall. She turns and flees, effectively taking my heart with her. She'll be able to put hers back together, but she'll forever own mine.

Something warm stirs me. When I blink awake, I groan and throw my arm over my eyes. Sun. Too bright. Too hot. Why the fuck are my shades open?

I roll over and nearly vomit. "Oh fuck," I groan again.

"Here. Try this."

I know that voice. But why the hell is she in my house in the morning? We broke up years ago. She hasn't been in my house since then. I feel the bed underneath me sink just a little as she sits down. I open my eyes, but immediately slam them shut when a headache stabs my brain.

"Fuck, shut the blinds."

"Sun will do you good. Take this. It will help."

"Shut the fucking blinds, Charlotte. Now." I leave no room for argument. When I feel her jump up and the room goes blissfully dark, I know my command worked.

Slowly, I open my eyes. Sitting on my nightstand is a bottle of Aspirin and red Gatorade. I reach for them, but don't move more than my arm. The devil knows if I do something more than that, I'll be losing the contents of my stomach. Though, what I feel sloshing around in there might be best to come out. I quickly take two Aspirin and wash it down with the cold liquid.

"Better?" Charlotte asks softly as she sits back down.

After chugging half the bottle, I set it back on my nightstand and slowly roll back over to my back. "Yeah."

I let my eyes fall closed as I throw my arm over them again. I just need a couple of minutes to remember what the hell happened last night. Clips of Lila rush through my head. How pretty she looked in that beautiful dress. How close I came to saying fuck it all and kissing her. The way her skin felt against mine.

But then, I see her tears. I can't remember a whole hell of a lot, but I know I was the cause. I put them there. Flashes of Charlotte hit my mind, and my eyes fly open. I let my arm fall to my side as I look at her. It's then I notice that she's completely naked.

I sit up, ignoring the screaming protests of my body; my exploding head. "What the fuck are you doing here?"

She flinches slightly and bites her lip. "A-after Lila saw us…"

I narrow my eyes as she trails off. "What, Charlotte?"

"Y-you asked me t-to come home with you."

I growl, but it's at myself. I remember bits and pieces of last night. Flashes of me slamming her against my bedroom wall as I ravished her mouth. "Tell me we didn't fuck," I demand.

She looks down. "I-I… can't…" She points to the floor.

I glance down and flop back on the bed. "Fuck." I close my eyes to try and rid myself of the image of the gold-foiled wrapper and very obviously used condom, but it only forces more and more images into my head.

Images of me slamming into Charlotte over and over again.

"Out," I growl.

"What?"

I don't need to see her to know her eyes are wide. "I said out. Call an Uber. Get your shit. And get out. You know fuck well that this never should have happened."

"Blake! You asked me here! You remember that?"

I open my eyes and shoot her a withering glare. "You know the rules! You know that while we both may help each other out from time to time, fucking always was and always will be off the plate!"

"We were both drunk! No one makes good decisions when they're drunk!"

My head is pounding.

My body is screaming.

But I throw off the covers anyway. I get out of bed and grab her by the arm, yanking her up with me. I drag her towards my bedroom door, grabbing her clothes on the way.

"Blake! Let go! You're hurting me!"

I do as she asks, but propel her towards the door anyway. "I'm not going to sit here and play this game with you. I won't even place all of the blame on you, Charlotte, because I had my own part in this." I open my door and push her out. I shove her clothes into her arms as I glare down at her. "But I know you weren't drinking. That's why I chose you last night. I trusted you to make sure I didn't do something fucking stupid. Like fuck you. That was my mistake. And you know I'll be talking to Elden about it because he should have been my backup. But this never should have happened. Out. Call an Uber. Go home. We're done. Friendship and everything. It's over."

"Blake!"

"Get dressed! Now!"

She flinches but does exactly what I ask her to. I grab my phone as she's doing it and pull up my app for Uber. We might be a small town, but people still like modern shit. Uber was the best fucking investment this town has ever made. At least to people like me who fuck up on this level and need to get women out of my site fast.

The other good thing about being a small town is that it doesn't take a long time for Uber to show up. We only have a few younger people who do it for extra money, but they seem to always be busy when they turn that app on. Thankfully, one of them was on today and was only a few minutes from my house. When he shows up, I've never been so thankful to see anyone in my life.

"You know you fucked up. No one in a uniform will go near your ass when I'm done with you."

She turns on the fake tears. "Blake, I'm sorry. You don't have to do this."

"It's too late. You may as well just move to another city because no one in Piper Falls is going to want you for a quick fuck or anything after I tell them you broke a promise we had between each other. No one is going to trust you won't do it to them. And you know damn well those friends of yours are going to side with the boys in uniform because that's all they care about. They'll turn on you so fast."

She glares. "You're such an asshole."

I shrug. "Like I said. I'll take my responsibility for my part in this shit. But you knew the fucking rules. I've never broken them with you. That's not what friends do. Betray one of us, Charlotte, betray us all."

Before she has a chance to respond, the Uber pulls up. I push her out the door and slam it in her face all without anyone seeing me in all my still naked glory. I lock the door and head straight for my shower. I turn the cold water on full blast before stepping under the spray. The water does everything it's supposed to. It wakes me up second by second.

And the more I come back to myself, the more I remember from last night. Including one huge thing that I would prefer to go on thinking never happened.

Elden wasn't the one who drove me and Charlotte here…

Chapter Seven

⊛ Lila ⊛

(Five Months Later)

I turn over and hug my pillow to my chest when the sun starts streaming through my window. I didn't sleep at all. Not even a little bit. Nothing new really. I haven't slept more than a couple of hours a night ever since the Fourth Fest when I saw Blake kissing Charlotte. It's very well-known that she has a thing for him. And even more well-known that it's strictly because he pins a badge to his chest. She's a badge bunny. Doesn't matter if it's a cop or firefighter. She's probably slept with them all.

I sniffle and squeeze my eyes shut against the tears that never stop falling, even when I'm convinced there aren't any left. I turn my face into my pillow and cry when the images burned in my mind play over and over again. Like a movie on repeat.

I was upset after Blake backed off once more just before I went on stage on the Fourth of July. I messed up the lyrics and embarrassed myself. I was going to confront him when I got off stage. I was angry he chose that particular time to let me down once more. But every time I looked at him, I could tell he was holding something back. I kept asking myself if maybe he's hiding feelings. I planned on talking to him as soon as I left the stage.

I didn't expect to see him wrapped around Charlotte the Slut. Seeing his hands all over her and his tongue down her throat made me completely sick to my stomach. I wanted to scream. Instead, I fled. Right into the arms of Blake's brother, Elden. He told me he'd come to get Blake, then noticed how upset I was. It was the first lie I've ever told him. I told him I was okay. Just didn't feel like my performance was the best.

Elden was supposed to have been working, so I was surprised to see him. Turns out, he wasn't feeling well and had taken the shift off but got a text from Blake asking him to pick him up because he was wasted. I don't know what happened, but when he asked me if I knew where Blake was, I lied a second time and said I hadn't seen him since he escorted me to the stage.

And from there, the lies just kept falling from my lips like bitter honey. When Keelan came up and hugged me and asked what happened, I lied again and told him I didn't know. Blake still hadn't shown his face when I was getting ready to leave several minutes later. But my heart got the best of me. Elden looked like death warmed over. So, I offered to drive.

Keelan agreed and took off. I guess Luke had texted him and asked if he could pick him up from Blake's since he drove his truck home for him. Elden and I waited for Blake. When he came out from the tent near the stage, he was grinning like an idiot and had his arm wrapped around Charlotte. I wanted to leave him there, but I simply couldn't.

When he realized I was the one driving, it was almost like regret flashed across his face. But it was gone so quickly, I was certain I imagined it. We all piled into Elden's truck. Thankfully, it was quiet. Blake kept his hands to himself, and so did Charlotte. Elden fell asleep after throwing up before we took off. I expected I'd be taking Charlotte back to her house. I didn't expect her to climb out of the truck after Blake and disappear inside his house.

That's when the tears started all over again, then never stopped. I took Elden back to his house and felt awful about how he felt. So, I stuck around and made sure he was settled. It was so late by that time, I just slept in his guest room. I didn't want to drive his truck home. I figured Keelan could come and get me the next day.

The past five months have been spent with me avoiding everyone. I haven't gone out with anyone. I've barely left the house. I didn't even go to the Halloween festival that Jaxon Walker throws. He has the best haunted house; the best corn maze. I love what he does for the community. It's why I always volunteer my time when he asks if I can do any performances or anything.

And those lies keep dripping off my tongue.

Even to my brother. My parents.

It's only three weeks from Christmas, my favorite holiday, and I'm not in the mood. I've done no decorating. I haven't even gotten into the festivities. We usually go shopping on Black Friday and put the tree up that night. We start decorating. Our entire block is lit up, but I didn't take part in any of it.

I jump at the knock on my bedroom door. I still live with my parents. I can't afford to support myself. My entire family wants me to concentrate on my dream of becoming a singer. Sometimes, I feel bad about it, but then I get on a stage and see the beaming smiles of my family and friends.

Of Blake.

I jump again at the knock and wipe my eyes. "Yeah?" I call softly.

The door opens slowly, and Luke pokes his head in. "Hope you don't mind. Your dad let me in."

I nod and bury myself in my pillows even more. Luke closes the door behind him and sits on my bed. He's the only friend I have right now. Faye is in New York and doesn't have time to listen to me whine. Adalle got a better job and transferred to Dallas.

It was like that night seeing Blake sent my life into a tailspin. Maybe it was already starting. It was just a month before that when I'd seen Daniel and his secretary. It seems fitting Blake destroy me in the same fashion.

I chuckle at myself. Yeah. Right. We weren't even together, so I have absolutely no right to be upset. None. Not even a little bit.

"I know about you and Blake."

I blink at him like he has grown two heads. "What?" I finally blurt.

He just nods and looks down at his hands. "Blake let some stuff slip a couple times."

I sit up slowly, still clutching the pillow to my chest. "Like what?"

He doesn't look up. "Let's just say, I know about everything. He spilled his guts on all of it."

My eyes just widen as my mouth drops. "No."

He nods. "Yep."

I hug the pillow closer and look down at my legs as I cross them.

52

"No one knows anything."

"I know."

I glance at him and take a breath. "I haven't told anyone because I didn't want to cause drama or anything. What do you know?"

"That you two are going back and forth with each other. And that he went about things wrong." He looks at me. "But that's not why I'm here. You've been hiding. No one seems to be able to get you out. I'm hoping you will for me."

I shake my head. "I'm not in the mood, Luke."

"Why? This isn't like you. It's been five months. You need to move on with your life. You're better than this. Everyone misses seeing you Friday and Saturday nights. I heard you haven't even been going into the bakery to grab your favorite treats. I know it's been rough, darlin', but we need to get you back to your fun-loving self."

I sigh. "You don't get it... I don't know what he told you, or what you think you know, but it's not easy to just..." I flail my hands around. "I'm so in love with him, Luke." I hug my pillow again.

He's quiet for a few moments before he takes one of my hands. "I think you need to talk, Lils." He squeezes my hand. "I'm not going to sit here and tell you what to do. But as someone you've considered family for your entire life, I'm giving you some brotherly advice. Come out with me tonight. Maybe we can get a couple of your other friends to come since Faye and Adalle aren't in town anymore."

I chew on the inside of my cheek. "You're not going to leave until I agree, are you?" It's a whisper.

"No. I'm not. Because this has gone on long enough. You either deal with me, or you deal with Keelan, who was close to being the one to show up here. And you know how that would have gone."

I sigh and flop onto my side, still hugging the pillow. "Unfortunately, I do. He's a bloodhound."

"Yeah, but he's going to have to know soon, Lils. You can't keep this from him like this. And keeping it all from Blake is doing no one any good at all. It's doing nothing but destroying you piece by piece."

I close my eyes and sniffle. "He could be honest, too."

"I agree, Lila. And it's also why I'm telling you that you need to talk. You can't keep avoiding each other like this. You're both so worried about how Keelan is going to react, but I'm telling you. This thing happening right now is affecting him more than anything else."

"Can I think about going out tonight?"

"Nope. It's one in the afternoon. You've been lying here all night and morning, by the looks of you. If you're not at Papi's at eight tonight, I won't be the one to pick you up. I'll send Keelan. Or worse... Blake."

My eyes snap open, and I throw a pillow at him. "Fine! I'll be there."

He catches the pillow and laughs. "You better be. You know I'm not playing."

I know him well enough to know he's definitely *not* playing. "I said I'll be there."

"Good." He puts my pillow back on my bed and gets up. "Be there."

I sniffle but smile softly as he leaves. The sun fades behind a dark cloud. My room becomes darker again as I close my eyes and allow thoughts of Blake to torment me once more.

火火火

His eyes. I know they're on me. I'm drowning, and I'm not even looking at him. We're on opposite ends of the table with a group of our friends, but I can still sense him; feel him. It's like he's sitting right next to me. I've done all I can to keep my mind off of him. I've even sung a song already. I've launched into a huge planning session for the next one with Leti and Dana.

None of it's helping. The only thing that seems to be doing me any good is the alcohol I'm downing. I know I've hit my limit, but I still drank one more in the hopes I'd get amnesia or something. It didn't work. I still remember my name, but I don't dare drink anymore.

"Ready for that song?" Leti, one of my friends who sometimes sings backup for me when I do the bigger shows, like the State Fair, asks.

"The DJ is signaling to us," Dana, another friend who does the same for me, says.

I wait a moment before answering. "Yeah. I think so." I don't feel dizzy. My head isn't pounding. I feel pretty good, actually. Despite the asshole sitting at the other side of the table.

Fuck him. He's not ruining me, my dreams, my passions, or my life. If he wants me to be done with him, then fine. I will be. It was pretty obvious, after I got to thinking about it, that that's exactly what he had intended. He wanted to hurt me enough to make me forget him. Well, it took me this long to finally be willing to do it, but I'll do it. No more Blake. No more dreaming of him and wishing he'd be mine.

"I'm so excited! We haven't performed together in forever," Dana says with a huge smile. I'll admit, her infectious happiness is helping me out a lot.

Leti takes my hand and drags me to the DJ booth. He hands us three microphones. We both hurry back to Dana, giggling. Truthfully, I miss singing. I haven't done a lot of it except for in my shower lately. Heartbreaking ballads that I've written and put in my portfolio. Songs I haven't put music to yet, but it's all in my mind. I just haven't really felt like doing more than write down the lyrics so I don't forget.

Stupid Blake.

Stupid me.

How could I allow him to affect me like this? The more I'm out, the more angry I become. No more heartbreak. No more sadness. Just anger. At him for doing what he did and me for letting it all drag me so far down.

"Ready?" Jason asks when the three of us reach the bar. He gives us a huge smile.

Dana nods enthusiastically. "So ready. We missed all of this."

I smile. I have, too. When I did my demo, I got some studio time. Me, Dana, and Leti even hired a band that we've become close to. We have a drummer, bass guitarist, and a lead guitarist who can play a rhythm guitar just as well. They even do the bigger shows that we go to with us. I had such high hopes for the demo we did together. We all did. We've heard nothing yet, but we're all still hopeful.

Even with all of the rejections we've been getting.

Jason helps us each up onto the bar, much to the surprise of everyone sitting at it. But even still, they all start to applaud with everyone else.

Except Blake, who is looking at me and around the bar like he might actually rip someone's throat out if they look at me.

You had your chance. You lost it. Maybe it wasn't the right time for us. Maybe it will be in another lifetime. But I'm tired of being hurt, Blake.

Words I wish I could actually say to him.

"Good people of Piper Falls," the DJ says with a teasing grin. "I give you Lila Rose with Miss Leti and Miss Dana singing some Miranda Lambert and Carrie Underwood. Give it for *Somethin' Bad About To Happen!*"

We all smile as the words come up on the screen, but we don't need to look at it. The three of us begin to sing in harmony.

> *Stand on the bar, stomp your feet, start clapping*
> *Got a real good feeling something bad about to happen*

The music begins and we all start a choreographed dance we've done countless times. It's a line dance that includes a lot of hip swaying sure to drive men wild. The music comes in and Leti starts to sing after a few beats.

> *Pulled up to the church, but I got so nervous*
> *Had to back it on up, couldn't make it to the service*
> *Grabbed all the cash underneath my mattress*
> *Got a real good feelin' something bad about to happen*

The three of us sing together as we play to the crowd, swaying our hips. My eyes fall on Blake. He's glaring at the crowd. I don't know what to make of him, but right now, I don't care. I start to sing.

> *Ran into a girl in a pretty white dress*
> *Rolled down a window. Where you heading to next?*
> *Said I'm heading to the bar with my money out the mattress*
> *Got a real good feeling something bad about to happen...*

We break into our line dance. Leti and Dana hit the lower notes and allow me the lead vocals as we launch into the chorus.

> *Stand on the bar, stomp your feet, start clapping*
> *Got a real good feeling something bad about to happen*

Drinks keep coming, throw my head back laughing
Wake up in the morning don't know what happened
Whoa... Something bad
Whoa... Something bad

I make my way closer to Leti and lean against her as I start my next part.

Now me and that girl that I met on the street
We're rollin' down the road down to New Orleans
Got a full tank of gas and the money out the mattress
Got a real good feelin' something bad about to happen

Dana grins wide and winks as she points to me and Leti and sexily struts towards us.

'Bout to tear it up down in New Orleans
Just like a real-life Thelma and Louise
If the cops catch up, they're gonna call it kidnapping
Got a real good feelin' something bad about to happen

We all turn and launch into our sexy line dance. Some of the guys at the bar are paying very close attention to us as they hoot and holler. It makes us perform briefly just for them. I wink at a tall blond that I haven't seen around before.

Stand on the bar, stomp your feet, start clapping
Got a real good feeling something bad about to happen
Drinks keep coming, throw my head back laughing
Wake up in the morning don't know what happened
Whoa... Something bad
Whoa... Something bad

As we had before, our harmonizing is perfect, but they allow me the lead. We each pick a guy and flirt through our dancing through the brief interlude as we sing before we launch back into our line dance.

Stand on the bar, stomp your feet, start clapping
Got a real good feeling something bad about to happen
Drinks keep coming, throw my head back laughing
Wake up in the morning don't know what happened
Whoa... Something bad
Whoa... Something bad

Blake's glare is burning a hole through the back of Blondie's head, but I'm not paying attention to him as the song ends. Blondie helps me down as the other two guys Dana and Leti were flirting with help them. The six of us make our way to the DJ and hand him the mics back. The crowd roars thunderously as the next person makes their way up to the stage.

The song is slow, probably a good idea. It will help calm people down. Blondie tugs me close, so we can dance. Other people join us on the dance floor laughing and smiling as they take a bit of a break after our rousing, hyped up performance.

"You were great up there," Blondie says. His hands are resting at my lower back. His voice is sultry, but not nearly as deep as I like.

As Blake's.

I inwardly growl at myself and lock my arms around him as I look up at him, ignoring the slight bit of dizziness. "Thank you. That felt good. I haven't performed in a while." I rest my head against his chest. It'll be good to calm down a little after performing. I'm not as drunk as I thought, but I can still feel the alcohol making its way through my system.

He's not as muscular as Blake. Not as tall. He doesn't smell like him. It doesn't feel as good to be in his arms.

I close my eyes. Good. Everything opposite. Even his eyes and facial hair. His facial features are softer. He has freckles and is clean shaven. Absolutely not Blake.

Not Blake at all.

"When are you getting a record deal?" he asks, his lips pressed against my hair.

I relax more and more into him. It feels good to have arms around me. Arms that aren't my brother's. Or Luke's. Or my parents.

Or Blake.

"Mmm... Trying. I have a demo in."

"They're fools if they don't sign you like yesterday."

I smile, though a little sadly. I tighten my arms around him as I sway with him. "Try over a year."

"That's fucked up. You should have a deal, Lila. Maybe you need someone who will fight for you a little. Get an agent or something." He runs his fingers through my hair, keeping me close with the other. I can feel his belt buckle against my stomach.

But that's not all.

He's hard as his belt buckle, and it ain't no zipper I'm feeling.

I pull back a little bit, but he doesn't let me. I look up at him just as his eyes widen. I tilt my head curiously, but before I know what's happening, Blake is pushing him back so hard that he falls into a table.

Drinks fly everywhere, but Blake is on him so fast that I barely have time to blink.

"Blake!" I scream.

But he doesn't hear me...

Chapter Eight

☆ Blake ☆

The more Lila sings, the more people pay attention. And the more of the men in this place pay attention, the more into the fucking song and dance she seems to get. Is it her friends that she's playing off of? Is she really that drunk? This is not Lila. She's never gotten up on the damn bar and performed like she's a fucking coyote from that stupid as fuck chick flick she made me watch with her once.

When the song ends, I'd never been so happy in my life. And considering how much I love her voice, saying I'm happy about her stopping singing is something I never thought I'd say.

It's obvious this little show is for me. It's punishment for the one I gave her. These past five months have been hard as hell, especially since I'm the one who caused her the pain I knew she was feeling. Everyone thought it had something to do with Daniel. They thought maybe the breakup and rumors had caught up to the strong exterior she portrayed. Especially since his company didn't go under as we all thought it would. Fucker is still thriving.

At least he's leaving her alone.

"You gonna be okay if we take off?" Keelan asks.

I raise an eyebrow at him. "Why wouldn't I be?" I give him a cocky grin. Best way to hide all emotions.

He laughs. "Yeah, you're right. You haven't had much to drink."

I shrug. "Just a couple. I'm heading out anyway." Because I don't want to see the fucker Lila is dancing with get any closer.

Luke grins. "Make sure Lila gets home."

I glare at him. He knows fuck well I won't be driving her home. Of course, he also knows I won't leave until she does, no matter how much it tortures me.

And hell if she thinks she's going home with that asshole. He's new to town and already has a shitty reputation. It was just last week that Jason almost threw him out of the bar. He left on his own without the girl he was trying to take home. Not that the son-of-a-bitch hasn't tried since. Lila is his new conquest, and I'm not going to let it happen.

Luke and Keelan take off along with a couple of other friends. They have plans that I didn't want to take part in. I don't even remember what they are.

I turn in my high chair and lean back against the table watching her. I don't care how many times I say or think that I'll leave in a few minutes because I don't want to see her dancing with another guy. I won't leave this bar before she does. I never have. I won't leave her to fend for herself. If Luke or Keelan aren't here, I will be. They both know that as well as I do. It's been an unspoken rule that's been in effect ever since Lila was old enough to come here.

I'm so fucked.

I watch as he pulls her closer. I can see how tense she is, even though she probably doesn't feel it herself. I know her well. It's when she tries to pull away from him and he doesn't let her that I'm on my feet and next to them before I even know what the hell I'm doing.

I shove him back from her while pulling her behind me at the same time.

"What the fuck?" he yells as he crashes into a table. Drinks fly everywhere. I feel bad about the woman and her friends who end up wearing their drinks instead of drinking them. I'll have to buy them a round.

After I kick this guy's ass for not only touching what's mine, but thinking he can make her stay near him when she clearly doesn't want to. Luke and Keelan are well aware of who this asshole is. It makes me question why neither of them stepped in and stopped this shit before it started, but I can't really bitch because I did the same damn thing and let him get near her.

No more. It ends now.

I reach down and pull him up from the floor. "You think you can just keep your hands on her after she tries to pull away?" I rear my fist back. All I can hear is the blood rushing through my ears. He flinches, preparing for the hit.

"Blake!" someone screams.

"Stay the fuck away from her!" I yell as my fist flies forward.

It seems an invisible force is holding me back. I fight it, but it's no use.

"Blake! Enough!" I'm physically thrown backwards. I stumble but don't fall. "Enough!"

I slowly come out of my red fog and see Lila looking at me with tears in her wide eyes. Her mouth has fallen open. Jason is escorting the asshole out of the bar. Everyone else is looking at me like I've lost my damn mind.

But none of them matter.

All that matters to me is Lila.

"Are you okay?" I ask her quietly as I step towards her. She steps back and shakes her head. Saying nothing, she strides out of the bar. I pinch the bridge of my nose and turn my attention on the girls whose dresses I just destroyed. "I'm sorry. Give Jason the bill. I'll pay for the dresses and get you new drinks if you want."

One of them shakes her head and smiles softly. "We saw her try to pull away. He tried the same thing with me last night. You should make sure she's okay."

I take a breath and nod as I look towards the door Lila is slipping through. "Get me the bill." I squeeze her arm gently and jog after Lila. I catch her just before she ducks into her car. "Lily, wait." I grab her door frame just before she slams it.

She glares up at me so fiercely that I feel the heat. And it's hotter than any fire I've ever fought. "Don't. You don't get to call me Lily. You don't get to call me Miss America. You don't get to call me Lils. To you, I'm just Lila. And I'd prefer you didn't even call me that because I don't want to see you or talk to you, Blake." The words are filled with venom.

While they cut me, they also fuel my anger. Anger I didn't even know I really had. I return her glare as I take her hand off her steering wheel and pull her into me. She tries to pull away, but I do the same damn thing that asshole did and hold her closer against my chest.

It might be the alcohol sloshing its way through my veins, but as her eyes widen while she pushes against my chest, it only fuels the fire.

"Do you have any fucking idea how hard this is for me, Lila? Huh? Do you know how hard it was for me to force my tongue down another woman's throat and wrap my arms around her when it was you I wanted to be touching?"

She scoffs and pushes harder, making me step back a step, but I don't let her go. "It was never something you had to do! Why couldn't you have just talked to me? Like an adult! Why hurt me intentionally like that?"

"Because there wasn't another way!" I yell back. "Because every damn time I'm near you, Lila, all I want to do is see if you taste like strawberries and cream like you did the night I kissed you!" I look up when Jason clears his throat.

"Take her somewhere else, Blake. You're drawing a crowd."

Both Lila and I look around. Jason is right. We have a lot of attention on us right now. Lila pushes me again, but I just tug her with me towards my truck and look at Jason. "Deal with her car."

"I'll keep the keys and lock up. You can grab it tomorrow."

I nod as I pull her past Jason. I tighten my grip on her hand even though she tries to shove me off. Her touch doesn't help the inferno fighting to burst free.

"Blake! Let go of me! What are you doing? You're fucking insane!"

I narrow my eyes as I round on her, not letting go of her hand. "I'm insane? Me?" I laugh. "You're the one who was out there practically fucking some guy you don't even know on the dance floor," I growl.

She punches me in the arm with a half scream that's adorable as fuck and goes straight to my dick. "You're such an asshole! I would never do that!"

I catch her other wrist and spin her so her back is against the passenger door of my truck. I press against her. "Sure as hell seemed like you wanted him."

She pushes against me again, trying to shove me off, but she's not going anywhere. She's pinned. Her perfect tits press against my chest. My dick strains against my jeans. I'm not sure when it hit full mast, but her body against me isn't helping.

"I've never wanted anyone like I do you, Blake. Never. How the hell are you so dense to not understand that?" Those tears are shining in her eyes again.

On its own accord, my lips lower so they're a hair away from hers. I press even closer, giving my cock much needed pressure.

But it's not enough.

Her against me is fucking never enough.

"Why, Blake? Why can't we be together?"

And just like that, the spell she has over me is broken. "You know the reasons, Lila." I step back, pulling her with me, and open the door to the truck.

"Forget it. Just let me go. I'll call Keelan."

"Right. And have him come after me for not taking you home? Fuck no. In the truck."

"What do you even care? You don't want anything to do with me. Just leave me the fuck alone. I can't do this anymore. I can't be friends with you and hold out hope that you'll start seeing me as more than just a little girl -"

"I don't fucking see you as a little girl. Get in the truck." I start to help her into it.

"Blake, stop it! Stop treating me like a little girl and just listen to me!" Those tears she's been fighting are getting dangerously close to falling.

"You know it's because of Keelan. No one is good enough for you. Not even me."

"I'm an adult! You can't make decisions for me and neither can he! I'm sick and tired of everyone treating me like -"

"Lila! Stop! Get in the fucking truck!" I grip her hips, but she grabs my shirt and pulls me into her.

I have no chance to react before her lips are on mine. The very thin hold I've been keeping on my control breaks. Instead of lifting her into the truck like I intended, I'm pushing her against it and grinding into her just as much as she's pushing herself into me. The hair on the back of my neck stands up. I know people are watching, but I'm struggling hard to care. That sweet taste, strawberries and cream, hits my tongue, and I'm gone.

I missed it.

I missed her taste. Fuck, I missed the feel of her in my arms while I ravished her mouth. I missed the way she opened for me and let me in. Everything she's doing right now. I missed all of it.

I missed her.

I force myself to pull away, but I don't want to. I want more. Maybe I'm not thinking clearly. Maybe I'm more drunk than I thought. Or maybe I'm just fucked up over her. All I know is I need more than a hot kiss. Anything less is like sitting in the depths of hell being whipped with fire.

"Get in the truck…," I whisper as she pants. "Please, Lila. Do what I say before I'm unable to stop." We're so far past that point. I wouldn't be able to walk away right now if all of the Budweiser Clydesdales were stampeding after me.

She looks up at me pleadingly before she does as I say. I help her climb into my truck and force my eyes away from how sexy her perky little ass looks in those Daisy Dukes she has on. But it doesn't stop my hand from sliding down her smooth, tan leg. I relish in the goosebumps I leave in my wake.

When she's settled, I close the door and look around. No one is paying attention to us anymore. In fact, there's no one out here anymore except one couple who I'd seen in Papi's. I adjust myself as I climb in the driver's seat and close the door. I let out a breath and rest my head against the headrest before turning to Lila.

"You're right. I can't do this anymore. Maybe it's because of the bourbon in my system, or maybe I just don't fucking care anymore."

She keeps her eyes on her hands as she sniffles. "I'm tired," she whispers. "So tired of this… No one has ever come close to you. I compare everyone to you. I just -"

I lean over and cut her off with a kiss that's far sweeter than the fevered one of seconds ago. My hand drops to her thigh as the other tangles in her hair. She sniffles and lets out a whimper that hits my heart harder than my still hard cock.

I pull back slowly. "I need to get you home, Lils. I don't want to ruin my Miss America," I tease with a grin that I know looks as conflicted as I feel.

She just nods and crosses her legs. I sit back and start to remove my hand from her thigh, but she holds it there. I glance at her but don't have the heart to argue. I start the truck and back out of the parking spot I'm in. I rub my thumb over her smooth skin but stop when I notice her legs are tightening.

We're blocks away from her parent's house. She moves my hand subtly but higher up her thigh. I let out a breath. "Lila. You're drunk, honey. And so am I. We can't do this."

"I'm so sick of everyone telling me I can't do things, Blake," she says quietly. Seconds later, she's climbing into my lap.

"Lila, fuck, what are you doing?"

"Maybe I need to be like one of those girls who chase all you firefighters around. Maybe then you'll finally understand how I feel about you and stop pushing me away." Her fingers spear into my hair and her lips crash against mine.

I barely have time to pull over so we don't end up in an accident. I know I'm not thinking clearly, but she for sure isn't. If my reflexes were what they usually are without alcohol coursing through my bloodstream, she wouldn't have made it to my lap. And she'd probably end up with a spanking for trying to do it while I'm driving. It's fucking dangerous.

But to hell with it.

I slam the truck in park and shut the engine off. I push my seat all the way back to give us room before wrapping my arms tight around her. I tangle my fingers in her hair just as her lips reach my neck and tug hard enough so she's looking at me as she grinds down on my dick.

"You're not one of them," I growl before taking her mouth in a hard kiss. "You'll never be one of them. You're so fucking far above them." I kiss her again, plunging my mouth into hers and starting a dance that she follows without effort.

"I wish I could make you see that no one compares to you," she whispers against my lips. Her hand finds my zipper, and I don't stop her as she drags it down.

"You shouldn't compare anyone to me. I'm not worthy of a woman like you, honey. I can never measure up."

Her small hand wraps around my cock as she pulls it out and starts slowly stroking me. If my nine inches wasn't hard as a steel rod before, it damn sure is now.

"All I've ever wanted is you. You're perfect."

Tears. Those fucking tears. They pool in her eyes, and I can't stand

66

them. I pull her in for another kiss as my other hand grips her and slides underneath her shorts to grip her perfectly round ass. I can't think. I'm dizzy, but I couldn't tell a damn soul if it's her or the alcohol. If I was placing a bet, my money would be on her.

She has me so close to coming, and all she's doing is touching me. She lets her hand fall from my shoulders as we both kiss each other like we need one another to breathe. I feel her pushing her shorts aside. I briefly wonder if she's wearing panties, but my cock is suddenly against her slick entrance.

We both fall against each other as she slams herself down on me.

"Oh fuck…," I groan. She's hot. So fucking wet. And so tight that she's squeezing my dick like a vice.

"Oh… God…" Lila's nails dig into my shoulders as she pulses around me. My other hand drops from her hair to her ass as she adjusts to my size.

I'm not small. I'm long and thick. There's no way that her or her tight pussy expected what's inside her right now.

I squeeze her ass and wrap my arms around her. "Lila, Jesus…"

"I… didn't…"

"I know, baby. Breathe…"

She lets out a breath before breathing back in. I run my hands up and down her back to help her relax as best as I can as she breathes. I tangle my fingers in her hair again and hold her as close as I can while I kiss her neck.

Her nails lessen their grip on me little by little, and Lila lets out another breath. "I don't care if I'm drunk," she says. "I just want you."

"You have me." I start moving inside her as slowly as I can.

There's no way I'd usually be doing this in a neighborhood in front of someone's house like this, but I don't give a fuck right now. All of my inhibitions are gone. All I care about is her and the fact that we should have done this a long time ago. Had I known how good she felt wrapped around my cock, I doubt I could've held back this long.

I kiss down her throat and nip it before I lick her. She moans low against my neck as she sucks lightly. She moves herself faster and faster over me until we're both panting and gasping for each other.

"Blake… Oh, yes!" She throws her head back as she twists her hips.

A small part of me still has some semblance of control because even though I want to see her tits exposed for me, I don't lift her shirt. I lean forward and kiss her over it, lavishing each of her nipples in turn, but I keep her the least exposed I can. I may have no control over the location I'm pounding into her pussy, but at least I still know enough to protect my girl from anyone seeing too much.

"Shh…, honey," I rumble commandingly. "We don't need anyone running out here because you're screaming." I grin against her neck and keep thrusting wildly into her heat.

I don't know what the fuck is happening. This is not something either of us would ever do, but maybe this is what we needed. Maybe it's what I needed to get my head out of my fucking ass. I know I want her. And I know damn well how she feels about me. The only thing holding me back is selfishness.

The sober part of me knows that's a fucking lie. The part trying to bust through right now and get me to stop fucking Lila in my truck three blocks from her parent's house where any number of people could see me railing her. He's not the part in control.

The part in control is the animalistic part. The part that is thinking of nothing more than how good she feels. How her pussy is getting wetter and wetter for me and tightening with each thrust. How she's squeezing my dick tighter as she rocks her hips against mine.

"Fuuuuuccckk…, Lily…," I rumble against her neck. Lily. No one else gets to call her that. Just like Miss America, Lily is my name for her. Faye can call her Lily Pad all she wants, but Lily is mine for her. All mine.

She hugs me even tighter as she bounces on me, meeting each and every thrust. "Blake, oh God… Please…"

"Christ," I whisper when I realize what she's asking of me. What she's so naturally asking me. My dick gets impossibly harder and thickens for her. She has no idea what she's doing, but I do. She's naturally submitting to all of me and my dominance.

Still keeping her close as I slam into her hard and deep, I slide my hand between us. I push her shorts aside a little more and rub my thumb against her clit in smooth fast circles. I give her the perfect amount of pressure as I rub.

Her head drops against my shoulder, and she bites just enough to make me moan. Her thighs tremble. Her pussy clenches tight around me. I know she's not going to last much longer and needs that command to reach the peak she's dangling off. She doesn't even know it's what she needs.

"Blake...," she moans, arching against me. Her entire body trembles.

"Come for me, Lila...," I whisper dominantly against her neck. I know it's my tone that sends her careening.

"Blake!" she screams into my shoulder, muffling herself. She comes hard for me, her hips bucking against me as I thrust into her pussy and rub her clit, prolonging her orgasm.

But it's not the feel of her coming for me that has that spark shooting down my spine and straight through to my dick. No. It's the fact that she was such a good girl for me and waited to come until I told her, and that she followed my command to stay quiet. I slam into her one last time, burying myself deep.

"Fuck..., Lila...," I groan as I come. My dick jerks inside as I fill her pussy with all of me, claiming her as mine.

As we both collapse against each other once more, this time to catch our breath, part of me wants to scream out loud to anyone listening that she's finally mine. That I'm the one for her. That she's the other half of my heart.

But that voice in the back of my head knows better. And he's the one who is screaming the loudest right now.

I've just crossed the one line I swore I never would, and it could cost me everything.

I'm so fucked.

Chapter Nine

☒ Lila ☒

Being in Blake's arms with him nestled inside me has my heart screaming. Finally. Finally, I have the man of my dreams. The only one who could ever own my heart. I hug him tighter, but everything that just happens crashes down on me.

I blush furiously and hide in his neck. "Oh God. Blake, I... I've... never just jumped at someone like that." What if after all of this time, I ruined it before it even began by throwing myself at him like that?

He chuckles into my hair. "I'm not complaining," he rumbles. But the words don't soothe me because the tone seems off. Not Blake. It's hesitant and nervous. And it causes me to slowly raise my eyes to his.

I bite my lip when his eyes don't meet mine. "Blake?" It's a whispered word I'm barely able to get out over the sudden lump forming in my throat.

I know it right away. I know I messed up. Blake has women throwing themselves at him all of the time. He's always said that when he finds his one, she won't be someone who does that. She'll love him for who he is and not the uniform he wears, and she won't throw herself at him. She'll be respectful of herself and her worth.

I always believed in my heart that it was me he was describing, but that all went out the window just now. I just did everything to him that he never wanted from anyone.

I take a deep breath and crawl off of him. He slides out of me, and

I instantly miss the feel of him. I smile softly as he helps me back into the passenger seat, but I say nothing as we both straighten our clothes. Blake packs his impressive member away, but the smile he had on his lips just seconds ago drops. The brief flicker of hope I had that I didn't mess this all up is gone.

I don't even know what to say.

Blake starts his truck once more and puts it into drive. "I shouldn't have let that happen, Lils. I'm sorry."

Lils. Not Lily. Not Miss America. Lils. It's almost as impersonal as Lila. Like we really are nothing more than friends. I hug myself. A lot of people close to me call me Lils. Keelan does. My parents do. Luke. But when Blake does it, he has to have a certain tone or it doesn't feel right. It feels like he's distancing me.

I guess that's exactly what he's doing. My whole body is still quivering and shaking for him. I still feel his come inside me slowly leaking out and soaking my panties. But it doesn't matter because I messed up.

Blake stops in front of my parent's house and sighs as he puts his truck in park. I don't look at him as I reach for the door handle. "You know this was a mistake," he says softly. So quietly that I almost don't hear him. "This shouldn't happen between us, Lila."

If I wasn't already quickly sobering, I would be at those words. I sniffle and nod. "Understood," I whisper as I slide out of the truck.

"Lila, I didn't -"

I turn and put on my bravest smile. "Don't, Blake. I understand. It was a mistake. I messed up. I'm sorry." I close his door and hurry to my door. My entire body screams at me to go back. To talk to him and work it out, but I propel myself forward and pray he doesn't follow. I don't want him to see me cry. I'm the one who messed up. Not him. It was my fault. Not his. Not this time, at least.

I hurry into the house and up to my room, thankful my parents aren't awake at this hour. I don't turn on any lights. I don't even look out the window to see if Blake is still out there. Instead, I crawl into the sanctuary my bed provides me and curl into myself.

There's no way sleep is coming to me tonight.

火火火

Your lips on mine
Content wrapped in you
The thoughts that run through my mind
They spin in yours, too

We're not meant to be
It's not our time
Took me this long to see
That there's nothing but pain over the line
Chasing time

I jump at the light knock on my door. The sun isn't even starting to rise yet. It's too early for anyone to be here. I put my song journal aside and make my way to my bedroom door, curiosity getting the best of me.

I furrow my brows when I see Keelan. "What are you doing here so early?" I whisper.

He raises an eyebrow questioningly. "Did you not see my truck parked in the driveway?"

I bite my lip and shake my head. "No… Sorry."

"It's fine. Are you crying? Why are you up so early?"

I shake my head and wipe my eyes. "I'm okay… Just didn't sleep."

He leans against the doorframe and crosses his arms over his chest. "I was really hoping the night out would do you some good. You looked like you were having a lot of fun."

I shrug. "I was, I guess." I look down at my hands.

"Lils, what's going on? I'm having a hard time believing this has anything to do with Daniel at this point."

I shake my head and huff. "Go, Keelan. I'm not your responsibility. Besides…, shouldn't you be at work by now?" I turn and head back to my bed, crawling under the covers and pulling them up and over my head.

"In a little while. And we're not doing this. You've known me your entire life. You should know me better than that. I'm not letting this go when I know something is going on with you." He shuts my door, and I

72

hope that means he's given up the fight and left.

Of course, I'm not that lucky. When has Keelan ever backed down when he's on the scent of my unhappiness?

The bed dips down behind me when he sits. I grip the covers tighter around me knowing what's about to happen.

As predicted, Keelan grips the covers and tugs them. Hard. I throw an actual tantrum that includes kicking and punching my pillow. "Just leave me alone, Keelan!" I snap.

"Not a chance in hell. Tell me what's going on. Does it have to do with Blake?"

I nearly choke as I whip my head around and stare at him in shock. "What?" I finally manage to squeak out.

He scoffs. "Come on. If you think I didn't notice the two of you gawking at each other all the damn time, you must think I'm stupid."

I just blink for several moments as I try to catch my breath. "It's… I… No… I'm…," I stammer.

"Lils. Just tell me. Because last night I was pretty sure you both were about to quit this shit and finally admit your feelings for each other to yourselves and everyone else. It's been years. Luke and I know. Our parents know. I don't know about Adalle and Faye, but I know Dana and Leti have their suspicions. So, what happened last night?"

I shake my head. "Wait. Luke?" I know he knows, but I didn't think Keelan knew that he knew.

"Okay, I don't know that he knows. I haven't actually talked to him. But I know that Dana and Leti know because they asked me a long time ago. I think mom and dad have always suspected. And I'm pretty sure Luke knows. He always seems to know things. Even if he doesn't let on that he does. Hell, I'm sure even Elden has his suspicions. Pretty sure Nick does. I think even -"

"Okay, enough. I get it." I hold up a hand and flop onto my back as I close my eyes. "Blake was my first kiss."

Keelan clears his throat. "Wow. Okay. Coming out swinging."

I'd laugh, but I don't have the energy. I'm tired of hiding it all. And if he already knows, then maybe it's best for him to know it all. "I was in love with him forever. I admired him long before that. You and Luke always treated me like I was an annoying kid. Always teasing me. I knew it was out of love, but sometimes, I guess I probably just got tired of it. Blake

73

was never like that. He always answered my questions. He never got annoyed with me being around. He'd tease me, but I always knew he never thought I was annoying like the both of you did."

"Blake is as patient as he is protective."

I smile softly. "Yeah. I know. I learned that early on. When I was sixteen, you know that my date to Homecoming ditched me for someone else, but I just went with Faye and Adalle."

"Yeah."

"Well, they were having a lot of fun. I wasn't. I was upset. Especially when Faye said she was going to take off, but that I could go with them. I knew the guy she was with was going to park with her. I didn't want to be the third wheel. I didn't want to call you because I knew you were busy that night. I called Blake and asked him to pick me up. I didn't want to go home. I didn't want to go with them. I just wanted to go for a walk or something and actually be around someone who seemed okay to have me around. Blake picked me up."

Keelan shifts so he's looking at me. "And that was the night of the first kiss. I remember how happy you were after that. And how shy you were around Blake."

I nod. "But it was never more than that. He was more friendly with me. But we'd agreed that it just couldn't happen between us. At least not then. I held out hope that when I turned eighteen, he'd change his mind. But he didn't. A best friend's little sister is forbidden no matter where you are. And I felt the same way. I thought you'd be pissed if you found out. I didn't want you to be mad at me, but I really didn't want you to hate Blake."

"Oh God, Lila. That would never happen. I've always held out hope that you and Blake would somehow end up together. I wouldn't be mad at all at either of you for that."

I open my eyes slowly and look at my brother. "Really?"

"Yeah. Really. Now, be honest. What's really going on?"

I sigh before propping myself up against my headboard. I focus on my blue comforter. "I've been keeping how I feel about him to myself," I start, keeping my voice low. "But after Daniel and I broke up, my feelings for him just came back so hard. Like they not only never quit, but they were stronger. More powerful and prevalent. At the Fourth Festival, Blake was being pretty attentive." I pause but decide to just plunge ahead. I've

74

already started. May as well just get it all out. "I thought he was going to kiss me. More than once. But I kind of ruined it before I went on stage. I asked him what was happening, and it was like a light went off or something. He backed off again and said that things just could never be."

"And then you went on stage and messed up. And told me you just didn't feel well."

I nod and play with a string on the comforter. "I wasn't really lying. I really didn't feel well. And I felt even worse when I got off the stage and saw Blake in the tent with his hands up the skirt of one of those badge chasers and his tongue down her throat. But it got even worse. Elden was supposed to take him home, but he was so sick. So, I took them home. And Charlotte went with him. I thought I was supposed to drop her off, too, like at her house, but she went inside his house with him. Elden was passed out. I cried the whole way back to his house."

"Jesus," Keelan rumbles. "It explains a lot. Blake mentioned that she should be one of the girls none of us in a uniform will touch because she went back on an agreement they had with each other. He didn't get into detail, but he was pretty pissed off, and everyone agreed."

"Good," I say softly. I don't really know what it all means, but maybe there's more behind that night. Maybe I'm hoping too much. It doesn't matter anymore anyway.

"I wonder if the agreement had something to do with helping each other out but nothing else happening. A few of us have agreements with a couple of girls. We consider them friends. Nothing else. But we'll ask them to help us out if something is going on. Like we have to go to an event or something and need a date but aren't with anyone. A few of the cops do that, too. Charlotte hasn't been seen in town for a while. Rumor has it that she went to live with a friend in Austin, but I never liked her so I didn't care."

"Serves her right." I flick my eyes towards him. I know he's pissed. He's not showing it, but I can tell. He's tense. Ready to strike. "That's not really all." I focus on the comforter.

Keelan sighs. "Okay. But this is the reason you've spent five months in hiding. Not because of Daniel, which is what you let everyone believe."

I shrug slowly. "It was easier than telling everyone the truth. Where would that have gotten us? You would've beat Blake up. And it would've solved nothing."

"I still might."

I smile softly and shake my head with a yawn. I suddenly feel so tired. With each spoken word, the weight I've been carrying seems to gradually lessen. I shift so I'm laying down again and snuggle into the pillows.

"It's not worth it. I don't want that. I've already ruined things." Tears sting my eyes. I take my journal filled with song after song about Blake Falcon and hug it to my chest.

"I doubt that." Keelan pulls my covers up and tucks me in, resting his hand on my hip.

"I messed everything up last night."

Keelan squeezes my hip. "I doubt that, too, Lils. But tell me."

I close my eyes once more and hug the journal tighter. "Please don't hate me. Or Blake. It wasn't his fault."

"What wasn't?" he asks quietly, his voice soothing me; lulling me.

"Last night... I..." I take a breath and let it out slowly. "I was upset with him... And I was pretty drunk... I think the alcohol I drank just took a little bit longer to have any effect on me. By the time I hit the dance floor, I was starting to feel it. There was this guy I was dancing with. I was about to ask him his name, but I got oddly uncomfortable. He was holding me against him super tight. The next thing I know, Blake is shoving him away from me, and Jason is pulling Blake off him before Blake pummels him. And then right after that, Blake is dragging me away from my car. I had no idea what was really going on."

"Sounds like he got involved in what could have been a mess."

I shrug a little. "Probably... From there..." I sigh and sniffle, curling into myself more.

"Lils, you're starting to scare me a little bit. What happened?" His voice has gone dominant, with the added effect of the tone he only uses with me when he wants information. A tone that never fails to have me spilling everything to him within seconds.

"I was frustrated. I was too drunk to drive, but not drunk enough to know what I was doing. I knew that, but I wasn't thinking straight. I was mad at him for stepping in after what happened on the Fourth. He was sober enough to at least understand what was happening. I was slower than that. We argued. Jason stepped in because there were a few people watching. Blake dragged me to his truck and told Jason to deal with my car. I was really mad at him for all of the pushing me away, and again... not thinking clearly...," I say defensively. Keelan is quiet, so I keep swimming right into the mouth of the shark. "We talked a little bit, and I threw myself at him not far from here..."

I can hear Keelan suck in a sharp breath. The silence is loud, but I should've given my brother the credit he deserves. Instead of screaming at me, like I deserve, he crawls into my bed behind me and hugs me close. I didn't know how much I needed it, and while all of the tension in my body releases, I cry.

He says nothing. He just gives me the support and comfort I need in this moment.

"I d-did the o-one th-thing he h-hates!" I cry. "H-he hates wh-when women th-throw themselves a-at him!" I cry harder. "I r-ruined everything!"

"No... No, Lila," Keelen whispers as he hugs me tighter. "You didn't mess anything up."

"I had to've! H-he sh-shutdown again, and t-told me it c-can't h-happen again!"

"It's not your fault," he rumbles soothingly. "It's not your fault."

I don't know how long Keelan hugs me, but I know it's long enough to make him late. Usually, I would care, but I find that while he holds me as I cry myself to sleep, I'm just glad I'm not alone.

Chapter Ten

⽕ Blake ⽕

I step out of the way as Nick comes barreling out the door at the station like his ass is on fire. "The fuck? What are you doing here?"

Nick chuckles. "Sorry, Cap. OT shift. Crew C needed some help. Your brother is in there, too."

"What happened? Where's Estrella?"

"She went home sick. Elden said he'd come in and cover her last few hours. I came in for Tiny."

"Sounds like chaos. It explains why you're running out of here so damn fast. Thought you had a hot date."

Nick laughs. "You know me better than that, Blake." He winks and hurries to his truck.

I chuckle and head into the station. I do know him. Nick doesn't stay in a relationship for long. And there's always a long time between them. Sometimes, it's fun to tease him about the longest relationship he's ever had being with a nice older woman who has a crush on him and always calls him to help her with things. Like getting her cat out of a tree. People joke about shit like that happening to firefighters thinking they aren't true. They are. Especially in small towns.

I make my way towards the Captain's office, nodding at a few of Crew C's firefighters along the way. When I get to the door, it's closed. I reach to open it, but Elden comes out with a scowl on his face.

I raise an eyebrow as I step back. "Dare I ask?"

"Don't. Don't do it. You'll only end up as miserable as me."

I bite my lip to hide the smile. My brother is the least dramatic person I know. If he's scowling, there's a reason for it. But it's also hilarious to see him off his game. "I'm asking. Only because I need to know since it's my shift coming in."

Elden shakes his head as he walks down the hall towards the bay. I follow him. "Just got back from a huge accident up the highway. State Patrol assholes had the whole fucking thing blocked up. We couldn't get through to get to the accident, but those fuckers bitched at us as soon as we did get there. I finally lost it on the dumbass they call a Sergeant when he started berating one of the guys."

I shake my head. "They've always been cocky fuckers. What else happened?"

"Not a lot. A few medicals. Nick's girlfriend's cat got stuck on the roof."

I laugh. "It's kind of adorable. She's a really sweet old lady. Even if she calls and we show up, she gives us the cookies she made for him."

Elden grins. "Pisses him off, too. He'll never admit it." Elden looks around. "Where's Murphey?"

"Probably looking for Luke. Fucker likes him more than me."

"I'll agree with that. You're unlikeable."

I try to grin, but it doesn't reach my lips. I look down instead. "Probably more accurate than I'd like to admit." I glance in the bay and see Crew C cleaning up and getting ready to leave as I lean against the wall and cross my arms over my chest. Luke is just showing up and heading to the locker room.

"What happened?" Elden mimics my position on the wall opposite of me.

I chuckle dryly. Trust my big brother to pick up on something being wrong. I swear he's part bloodhound. "Things last night got fucked up quick. I've kept it to myself, but I've had a thing for Lila for years. I was her first kiss. It never went further than that. Not that I wished it wouldn't have. She's the girl of my dreams. Probably why I've never settled."

"Makes a lot of sense, actually. Go on. What happened?"

I give him a look but don't question. Fucker has probably been talking to Luke and knows everything. "Well, I've been doing a damn good job at keeping her at a distance, but it's been getting harder. The thing with Charlotte had to do with Lila. You were sick, so you don't really know how upset Lila was, but I got Charlotte to help me out that night. I kissed her in front of Lila. Charlotte played her part. I woke up the next morning with Charlotte in my house."

"You drunkenly fucked her."

"Yep. But I had a deal with her. No fucking. Just two friends helping each other out of sticky bullshit when it's needed. A couple years ago, she asked me to help her with a County cop who wouldn't leave her alone. There were a few other things. She has done the same for me once or twice. It was a mutual agreement that she broke. She wasn't drunk. But I didn't trust her fully. It's why I called you."

He rubs his head and shakes it. "Blake, fuck. Is this why Lila was so quiet these past months?"

I nod miserably. "Yep. That's on me. But I thought she'd get over it. Last night, I found out how wrong I was. And I found out I'm nowhere near in the position to get over her. All it took was seeing some asshole's hands on her, and I was seeing red. He's not a good guy, so that worked in my favor, but I might've been calling you to come bail my ass out had Jason not stopped me from kicking his ass. And before you start lecturing, it don't end there. I took her home after arguing with her, and fucked her in my truck three blocks from her parent's house."

Elden's eyes almost bulge out of his head, and he nearly chokes. A couple heads turn our way, but I shoot them a glare, and they scurry. "What the fuck is wrong with you?" Elden asks.

"The real question here, is why did I proceed to tell the woman of my dreams after I fucked her that there's no way it can happen again?"

"Christ." I see his eyes flick to the bay. "You're about to answer to Keelan. And he looks like he's about to feed you you're fucking soul."

I turn just in time to see Keelan. Right before he pushes me so hard that I almost fall to the floor. "Keelan! Wait a second!" I bark at him as I steady myself.

"Did you think I wasn't gonna find out? Huh? You think I'm fucking stupid or something?" He shoves me again, but this time, I'm ready for it.

I block the shove and take a step back to brace myself. "Let me explain!"

"Explain? Explain why my sister cried herself to sleep in my arms? Or explain why you kept your feelings for her hidden all of these years? Why you kept it from your best friend! Want to explain that?" He tries to punch me, but I block it.

"Keelan! Enough!" I snap. "I'm not fighting you!" I level him with a glare. "Let me fucking explain!"

"Fine! Don't fight me! I could give a fuck less if you fight back or not!"

My eyes widen when I see a couple of crew arriving for our shift. Elden backs them up with a smirk, but does nothing else. I'd level my glare on him, but I'm too busy making sure Keelan doesn't land a punch.

He doesn't even bother with one. Instead, he goes in for a tackle any linebacker would be proud of. He takes me to the ground, my back crashing into a door behind me. We fall through it into the locker room.

"What the hell?" Luke yells in surprise, jumping away from the door. Murphey scurries and barks.

"How, Blake?" Keelan screams at me, his fists bunching my shirt.

I grip his arms and shove him off me, quickly jumping to my feet. "Stop, Keelan!" I command.

I didn't expect him to. He comes at me again. "How the hell could you love her so much and treat her like that?"

For the second time in seconds, my eyes widen. "What the hell are you talking about?"

"You know what I'm talking about, you son-of-a-bitch!"

"Enough!" Luke barks, stepping between us. He shoves Keelan back just before he reaches me. "Stop! You're fucking brothers! Act like it!"

Elden appears by the door. "You two want to take it to the office so the rest of the crew can get ready to come on or leave?"

I give him the glare I've been waiting to but don't say a word as I push past him and towards the office. I can hear his laugh following me the entire way. Seconds later, Keelan and Luke step into the office behind me.

Keelan slams the door behind him and gives me a vicious glare. I prepare myself for another attack. "You know what pisses me off the most, you asshole?"

Not like I've never been called an asshole before, but that one hurts. I swallow a little harder than I intended. "Keelan -"

"Shut-up, Blake. I'm so tired of every damn thing that comes out of -"

"Both of you, knock it off!" Luke cuts in. Both of our eyes snap to him. Out of all of us, Luke is the calmest. He gives off a don't give a fuck attitude. Nothing ever really bothers him. When he gets pissed, though, everyone needs to watch themselves, because he doesn't take anyone's shit. "You're both acting like this entire thing is all on Blake, and it's not." He points at me. "Not to say you didn't fuck up because you royally did. Not being upfront and honest with Keelan in the first place is completely on your shoulders and Lila's."

I sigh and drop into the chair behind the desk. "I -"

"Stop it," Luke commands. "Not done." He rounds on Keelan, who is still standing, and looks him directly in his eyes. "And you. It's no wonder Lila and Blake never came to you on this. Look how you're acting? Exactly as they both feared you would. He sacrificed his happiness and broke Lila's heart fuck knows how many times now so he wouldn't lose you. So Lila wouldn't be put into a position where she'd have to choose between him and you. So, sit down. Shut-up. Talk about this like the men and brothers you both are. And when it's all out in the damn open, accept what we've *all* been waiting to happen because this crap is ridiculous and has gone on long enough." He gives me another glare as Keelan sits down, thoroughly put in his place, as I am. He walks out the door and slams it behind him.

"Shit," I say looking after him.

"We deserved that."

I lean back in my seat and sigh for the fiftieth time. "Look, Keelan -"

He holds up a hand. "Just let me talk first. At least then you'll know why I'm so pissed."

I nod. "Okay."

"I'm pissed because you both have been hiding this because you think I'd be pissed off about it. I'm not pissed at that, Blake. What upsets me the most is that you both think that little of me to think for a second I'd stand in the way of your happiness."

I look down at the desk. "Guess I called it wrong."

"Damn right you did. And it cost you both years and years of hurt and pain. I know how protective I am of her. Fuck, we all are. And I know

I come off as this asshole who thinks no one is good enough for her. But dammit, Blake, it's never been like that with you. You've always been so different with her. When Luke and I thought she was annoying as hell, you were sitting there with her helping her with her homework or explaining how something works on your car. You never got annoyed with her. I wasn't blind. I saw how much you cared for her. We all saw it. I never said shit about it because I didn't want to make a fool of myself. And I never saw either of you acting as more than friends, even though I suspected and did see a lot of gawking and longing. Maybe that was naive of me. Or maybe you were good at hiding it. That's why I'm pissed. I'm angry as hell because neither of you were honest with me or each other. And I'm livid that you think that low of me to ever dream I'd be the one to stand in the way of love."

The whole time he's talking, I'm understanding a lot more of where he's coming from. It makes me feel more and more like shit. After a few moments of him staring me down, I finally find my words as I look up at him, meeting his eyes once more.

"First, I'm sorry, Keelan. I don't know how to really explain that it wasn't my intention to make you feel like I thought down about you. I don't. I really don't. You're my best friend. Hell, you're as much family to me as Elden is. And it's for that reason alone that I held back. I never wanted things to get awkward with us, but I certainly never wanted things to come between you and Lila. I know the high standards you have for the man who wins her heart, and I don't meet them. I don't come close."

"Blake, come on. Are you really that stupid?" he interrupts. I close my mouth. "I was describing you to a tee. An honorable man who is protective of her. Someone trustworthy who would treat her like a queen and worship the ground she walks on. Someone who will support her and love her; pick her up when she's down on herself and feels like she can't make it. Someone who will listen to her and be everything she needs. Her real life superhero. You." He gestures to me.

I swallow as I stare at him in complete disbelief. "I'm a fuck up. How many times have you told me I'm a complete mess?"

He crosses his arms over his chest. "How many times have I said Lila makes you better?"

His words cut me deep because he's right. As if every single conversation he and I have ever had over the course of our entire lives is playing like a movie in fast forward through my mind, I can suddenly see very clearly that he has spent a lot of damn time pushing me towards her. And like the fuck up I am, I made an absolute mess of things, as I usually do, and wasted so much precious time I could've spent loving her.

How many heartbreaks could I have saved her from? And how many of those heartbreaks were caused directly by me and my actions? I'll take the blame for all of them because they're all my fault. I could've saved her from Daniel. I could've saved her from seeing me with Charlotte. I could've saved her from each and every heartbreak she probably went through every fucking time I walked away.

"Why didn't you say something?" I finally ask. "When I wasn't taking the hints, why didn't you just tell me?"

He shrugs and looks down. "Man, I don't know. This whole thing is just messed up. I wish we could all go back in time and just start over." He looks up and grins teasingly. "Maybe I would've punched you the second time around."

I laugh, and it feels good. The tension that tightened my muscles slowly breaks free, but the happiness quickly dies. "Fuck, about last night…," I start.

Keelan shakes his head. "Don't. I already know. And I'm not even mad. At least you both got it out of your system. Just figure out how to fix this shit with her. And quit thinking I'll be such a dick like that."

I breathe a sigh of relief and look at my watch. "Fuck, I need to finish with Elden and brief the team." I stand.

Keelan does the same. I round the desk and pull him in for a hug. "I'm sorry, man."

"No hard feelings." He hugs me back. "But you're gonna have your work cut out for you with Lila. She thinks she made progress with you but fucked up because she jumped you like our average, run of the mill badge bunny would. She knows one of your biggest things about finding your one is that she won't be someone who acts like that."

We let go of each other, and I pinch the bridge of my nose. "Christ. That could never be something I'd think with her. I fucking jumped her just as much."

I follow him out of the office. I have to take my mind off Lila and put myself into firefighter mode, but it's not easy when all I can think about is fixing everything I did wrong with Lila and making up for lost time.

Before we make it to the guys, my phone chimes. My heart leaps into my throat. I almost expect it to be Lila telling me she wants nothing to fucking do with me, but that's not what it is at all.

James Maxton: Got good news. I know it's early, but this can't wait. Call me when you can.

I halt in my tracks and wave Keelan on. He knows what I need from him. He'll talk to Elden and get our team ready for our shift while I make my call.

I duck back into the office as he answers. "Blake! Good news, man. We went back and forth with things that you requested and had it looked over by the lawyer you specified. I think we have a solid offer and contract here, man. I emailed it over to you."

"Let me get into my email." I sit down at the desk and quickly pull up my email. I find his email and start looking through the offer and contract. After a few moments, my grin is widening. "Dude, I really think this is ready to present to Lila."

"Think she'll sign it?"

"You'll have to give me a few days. I'm on shift. But yeah, man. I think this is good. I think she'll sign it. We'll need to set up a meeting with you and the lawyers. She'll want some of her family there."

"Anything she wants. I'll get it done."

"And you'll be her manager? She's not going to get handed off to some young asshole trying to make a name for himself in the business?"

"Yes, sir. That's in her contract. I've been named as her manager. I'll be there at the signing. I'll need to sign, too."

"I know it's unprecedented to do shit this way."

"Hell. It'll be fun. Get me back to my roots."

"I want someone she can count on out there. Not someone who has the company and money at heart."

"I know, Blake. We've talked extensively over the past few months about this. She'll be in good hands. Her and her band. VIP treatment. We know talent when we see it."

I nod. "Set up the meeting for next week. Work with our lawyer for a meeting time. I'll text you my schedule."

We say our goodbyes and hang up. For the first time in years, I feel good about what's coming. I know I have a lot of groveling to do, but

85

I'm more than ready to put all of this behind us and look to the future. And make up for so much lost time.

Chapter Eleven

 Lila

(Two Days Later)

"Lila! Hurry up!" Keelan yells up the stairs. "If you're late, I'm going to get my ass kicked!"

I glare at my door as I open it but hurry out anyway. "What is the deal?" I hurry down the stairs.

Keelan paces impatiently as he looks at his watch. "Secret. Are you ready? Let's go." He takes my hand and drags me after him. I look at both of my parents in utter confusion, but they both just grin at me.

"Keelan, what's going on?" I try to yank my hand free, but I know I'm better off not fighting.

"Just trust me." He practically throws me in his truck. I squeak as he closes the door and rushes around to the driver's side. He pulls out of the driveway and practically speeds away.

"Keelan! Slow down! What are we doing? Where are we going?"

"You'll like it."

I huff out a breath and fold my arms across my chest. I've gotten nothing out of Keelan. Nothing. At all. Not even a hint. He got off work this morning and didn't even bother going to his own house. Nope. He showed up at our parents and took his shower before getting dressed. Then he woke me up with breakfast and told me to hurry up and eat it.

I was so dazed and confused, I just did what he said without question. When I was finished and sort of awake, I asked him what was going on. He just told me to get dressed in jeans and a t-shirt with some cowboy boots. He even commanded I tie my hair back.

I don't have a clue what time it is. I have no idea where he's taking me. I feel like I'm being kidnapped. And the kidnapper is my idiot brother. I huff again.

Keelan laughs. "Just trust me."

I shoot him a glare. "I'm not speaking to you. I don't even have my wallet or purse."

"Don't need it."

"Yep. I knew it. You've tired of me and are taking me to the slaughter house."

He laughs again. "Not the slaughter house. Just trust me."

"I don't. I have no trust in you. You're a madman."

"Well, that I can't deny," he drawls.

"Ugh." I turn away from him and look out the window. He's heading for Walker Estate. I narrow my eyes as I try to think of why he'd be heading there.

I'm unable to come up with a single reason. I usually sing at the Christmas Festival, but that's still three weeks away. I know they're doing setup for it, but Jaxon Walker always has all of that taken care of before I ever enter the picture.

Sure enough, Keelan pulls into Walker Estate. I shoot him another glare as he stops. Jaxon grins as he heads for the truck.

"What are we doing here?" I demand.

Keelan shrugs. "Have fun." He shoots me his stupid cocky grin as Jaxon opens my door.

"I'm not leaving this truck until you tell me what's happening, Keelan," I seethe.

He just keeps smiling. "I'll just have Jaxon pick you up and carry you out."

I glare viciously and am just about to argue when I see the devilish look in Jaxon's eyes telling me that he'll totally drag me out of the truck. I stomp my foot. "Ugh!" I jump down.

Jaxon closes the door and holds out an arm as Keelan leaves, honking his horn on the way. "I think you might like what we have going on today."

I look up at him pleadingly as I place my hand on his arm. He starts escorting me to the stables. "Jaxon, please tell me what's going on."

"I can tell you that your horse awaits."

I blink at him. "That... brings more questions to light. Why a horse?"

"Because it's easier than driving," he drawls with a half smile and wink.

I shake my head. "I swear. Whatever you and Keelan have going on is..." I trail off because I can't find the words.

Jaxon laughs. "I think you'll have a lot of fun. When you get to your destination, there will be a nice surprise that awaits you." He walks me to the stables as I sigh but stops short. "Just head in. Caleb is in there. He's got everything ready to go."

"Hopefully some damn information...," I grumble as I continue walking. I hear Jaxon laughing as he heads back in the direction we came. I only take a few steps before stopping in my tracks.

"You know it's gonna be your turn soon." Blake's voice is deep and sounds so velvety. I didn't realize how much I missed hearing it in more than just my head. Even if it has only been a couple of days.

I bite my lip and stay out of sight.

Someone laughs. "Sure. Find me a man that's handsome, dominant, and looks deliciously rideable while wearing my Stetson. I just might believe you then."

Blake laughs. "I'll get right on that."

There's a few beats of silence, but I can hear them moving around. The horses make chuffing and neighing noises. Blake quietly soothes one of them.

Still completely unsure what's going on, I take a deep breath and make my way inside the stables. Once more, I stop in my tracks. Caleb is brushing down a horse, but he's not what draws me. It's the man who never ceases to stop my heart; to completely take my breath away.

Blake.

He always looks mouthwatering, but today, it's so different. He's wearing a short-sleeve, button down, western-style, dark blue shirt. His blue jeans are worn out and fading. There's even a small tear on his thigh where the fabric wore thin. They're my favorite pair of jeans that he wears. As if that wasn't enough, though, he had to throw in the worn, brown leather belt with the buckle his dad gave him with his initials. Another thing he knows is my favorite.

His bulging arms look like they're stretching out the material of the shirt even more than his sinful torso does. I know underneath his clothes, he's pure muscle. I also know that the tattoos on his arms do nothing to hide the sexy veins and toned muscles he has.

On top of his head is his worn out brown Stetson, the one that matches mine. His bootcut jeans are pulled down over his brown leather cowboy boots. Attached to his waist and covering his so sexy ass is my Stetson… the one that matches his.

My breath hitches.

Blake looks over at me with a huge grin as he feeds the black Stallion an apple. "'Bout time you showed up. We were getting a little antsy."

I force my feet to move as Caleb saddles up the sleek chestnut colored mare he'd just been brushing. "What's going on?" I ask quietly, unable to meet his eyes. I'm still beyond embarrassed about the way I jumped him.

When I reach him, Blake cups my chin in his palm and tilts my head up. "Thought we could go for a ride. We haven't done this in a while." He brushes his thumb across my lower lip, and I melt. But when he leans in for what I'm sure is supposed to be a kiss, I shake my head and put my hands on his chest.

"What are you doing?" I whisper.

"Apologizing," he rumbles low. His other arms snakes around me and pulls me closer. "Apologizing, Lily. I fucked up. I know I did. And I'm trying to make up for it."

My heart stutters to a stop in my chest before it picks up pace and tries to jump out of it. I want to believe he's saying what I think he is, but my brain is screaming at me that he's not being serious. That in five seconds, he'll back away again and break me for what will be the final time. I can't do it anymore. I can't keep piecing myself back together after he shatters me, inadvertently or not.

I love him. I'm so in love with him.

Which is what makes me push against him a little more as I shake my head. "Blake, I… can't… do this anymore…" I look down when his grip only tightens on me. I knew he wouldn't let me run. "I know I upset

90

you the other night. I should never -"

"Baby… Stop… Stop…" Blake pulls me even closer to him. I've always loved his hugs. They're as comforting as he is. "Lila, I know you think you're the one who messed up, but you didn't. You didn't do anything wrong. I did. And I've been wrong for years." His fingers run through my ponytail as he sways gently with me while he hugs me.

Tears sting my eyes. He's saying everything I've longed to hear from him. But how can I trust that he means them this time? Do I have the strength to give him another chance? God, I really want to…

"It took me a long time to realize just how badly I'd fucked up, but I'm hoping you'll give me a chance to at least try and redeem myself." He tugs my hair just enough so I'm forced to look up at him.

I give in to the silent command, but I sniffle. "I don't know what to say…"

He smiles softly down at me. "You don't need to say anything, baby. They say actions speak louder than words, so let me show you that I mean it when I say I'm all in. I have a lot to prove and make up for. But I'm willing to put in the work if you're willing to let me try."

I search his gorgeous dark depths for several moments before finally taking a breath and nodding. I close my eyes and reach up to wipe a stray tear before opening them again. I stare straight ahead, which is to his chest.

"Okay…," I whisper. "But the other night -"

"Wasn't your fault. And we'll talk about it all on the way to our destination. I have a surprise for you."

He moves his hand from my hair, down my arm, and to my hand. The other falls from around me when I take his hand and let him lead me to the mare that's already saddled and ready for me. He kisses my forehead just before he helps me up into the saddle. I settle.

He squeezes my thigh. "I'm gonna fix this," he drawls deeply as he looks up at me. He takes my hat off his belt and reaches up to place it on my head.

I adjust it with a soft smile. "You're not the only one to blame. I -"

He shakes his head. "We're not playing that game. We're just moving forward."

Moments later, we're both riding out of the stable. Blake is on the black Stallion. We start at a leisurely pace as we head out across the field.

After a little while, Blake makes a turn onto a trail that I've never been on.

"Where are we going?" I ask curiously. "I haven't been on this trail before."

"I've come out here a few times. Mostly when I need to think. It leads to an outlook that has a giant tree I think has been there for centuries."

I nod as I fall in step next to him again. The trail is wide. It looks more like a trail for four-wheelers than for horses. Looking ahead, though, it seems like it will be a gorgeous journey. The trail is green and grassy. Flat, for the most part. There looks to be a bit of an incline off in the distance.

What seems like hours upon endless hours of silence, I finally take a deep breath. "I really am sorry. I feel like I forced your hand."

"You didn't force anything."

I give him a dry chuckle. "Pulling you in for a kiss... Then grabbing your dick after I straddled you in your truck while you were driving because I'm apparently incapable of being mature. And then shoving it inside me and riding you in the wide open... Yeah, sure. That's not forcing anything."

Blake laughs. I shoot him a pouty glare. He just gives me his cocky grin. "Lila, I told you I wasn't complaining, baby. You have no idea how many times I've imagined what it would be like with you. And all of the ways and places I'd take you. My truck included."

I peek at him, blushing furiously. He doesn't look at me, but I can see that sexy grin on his lips. Just that look soaks my panties and makes me squirm a little in the saddle.

New subject is necessary.

"What brought all this on? Why the sudden change?"

Blake sighs. "Keelan and I talked, but that's not really all of it. I mean, it makes me feel better that he's not going to be upset or hurt. That there isn't going to be tension and awkwardness between us all. Mostly for your sake. But the biggest reason is because I'm tired of this. I'm sick of fighting it. Keelan and I got into a bit of an altercation, but I had already decided I was done with this. The night in the truck was sort of the nail in my coffin. I couldn't walk away from it this time. I tried, but I knew it wouldn't have lasted."

"He knew," I say quietly. "I mean he didn't know about the kiss

92

and everything... He knew our feelings for each other, though. Or at least suspected yours. He knew mine. I hadn't said a word."

"We had a good talk over the course of our shift. Your parents' feelings about all of this. His. Where I wanted to take this. How serious I am."

After a few more moments of silence, I steel myself and look up at him. "I almost packed up and moved this time. To Dallas."

His head snaps to mine. His eyes are on fire, even though his face portrays the shock he obviously feels. "What? Why?"

I shrug before looking back out over the trail. "Because over the past few years, I've been pretty up and down with you. I thought we'd finally be together by the way you would act. Then, it was like it all changed in seconds, and we were back to being nothing. Like a lightswitch. One second, we're on. The next, we're off. But when it really started to hurt was the night before the Fourth. Being with you after I sang that song. And you just hugging and supporting me. Then, at the Festival... The almost kiss..." I trail off as the tears sting my eyes once more. I reach up to wipe them away as I shake my head.

"I'm sorry, Lila. I know how badly I fucked up. I know I did it again and again. It took me a long time to see it, but it's all clear now. Everything with us. How messed up I let it all get." He reaches over and nudges my horse to the left just after we reach the crest of the incline. "No more. I'm going to show you just how sorry I am for all of it. And I'm going to make up for all of it as long as you'll let me."

Keeping my horse next to his, he leads us both to a secluded lookout point that looks over a small river basin. I gasp as we come into the clearing, and I'm able to see the beauty that captivated him enough to make this his place to come to for quiet.

There's a giant Desert Willow tree growing. It's the tallest I've ever seen, and I've never seen one anywhere other than someone's garden. I stare at it in awe as Blake drops down from his horse. He helps me down, but my eyes are totally on the tree as I slowly walk to it.

"Oh God... It's beautiful...," I say, barely above a whisper. I reach up to touch one of the delicate leaves. It's December, so it's not blossoming, but it's still as beautiful as ever.

Blake's arms wrap around my middle, and he pulls me back against his hard body. His lips are warm against my neck. "It defies the odds. It shouldn't be here. But it is. Withstanding everything. Still tall and proud."

"It's impossible."

He smiles. "I think it likes telling everyone that impossible or not, it can be done." He kisses my neck before taking my hand and pulling me down.

It's then I notice the blanket under the tree. There's a picnic basket on it and a small cooler. Suddenly, I'm starving. I don't know how long the ride was for sure, but I know it was a couple hours, at least.

Blake settles me between his legs and sets the picnic basket between mine. "Open it."

I look at him questioningly as he opens a bottle of water. He hands it to me after taking a drink of it. I take a long drink and hand it back to him as I open the basket.

What I expect to see is some kind of food. I don't really know what, but something. That's what picnic baskets are for, right? I don't expect to see papers neatly stacked, held together with a large paper clip, and tied with a pretty dark pink bow, my favorite color.

I tilt my head. "What is it?" I take out the papers and start untying them. Blake doesn't say anything, but his arms wrap around my waist. He rests his chin on my shoulder after kissing it.

I flip the papers over in my hands and stare at them.

Before I know what's happening, my mind is computing it all at a million miles a second. I can't keep up.

I blink a few times as I look through the pages in silence. It's not that I don't want to speak. It's that I can't find the words.

A contract?

A contract!

"Blake…"

"When I went to that training before the Fourth, I ended up next to a record exec or something on the plane. He works with Destiny Records. We got to talking about you. I showed him a video I have of you on my phone. He asked me for a demo. Keelan helped me get it. We've been in talks for a few months ironing this out. He's going to be your manager. Well, that's if you consent to it. He got you one hell of a deal. Music is all yours. You have creative freedom. They already picked out thirteen songs that they love. The decision is ultimately yours, but I got us a meeting with the attorney, Keelan, and your parents later tonight at my house to go over all of this. Just so you and everyone understand exactly what you'd be giving and getting."

"Oh God," I gasp out. "Blake this… Oh my God!" I drop the contract back into the basket.

For the second time in a couple of days, I jump Blake. Only this time, it's completely different. I wrap my arms around him and kiss him so deeply and passionately, with all that I am, that it's impossible for him or me to doubt how I feel in this moment.

Ecstatic.

Hopeful.

And so head over heels in love with the man underneath me with his tongue in my mouth and arms wrapped tightly around me. The man who has just dedicated himself to making my dreams come true.

We kiss and make the most beautiful love underneath the Desert Willow until we're forced to release each other and ride back to Walker Estate in order to be back in time for the meeting.

With him beside me as we take the first steps to our future, I know it's looking bright.

Chapter Twelve

☯ Blake ☯

(Nine Months Later)

I step out of the shower in the locker room at the station after wrapping a towel around my waist. We have separate locker rooms for men and women, but I still don't need the guys I work with seeing me naked.

Lila on the other hand…

A slow smile creeps over my lips when I see her perched on the counter near the sinks swinging her feet. "Not that I'm complaining at seeing a beautiful woman hanging out in the locker room at four in the morning, but what are you doing here, baby?" I start drying my hair with another towel.

"Missed you."

I chuckle and grin even wider. Lila and I have been happy and going strong ever since the day I gave her the contract underneath our Desert Willow. She ultimately signed the contract. She finished recording her album and did a short summer tour around the United States opening for mega successful superstar, Gracie Rian. She fangirled the whole time.

I stalk to her and step between her legs when I reach her. I wrap my arms around her waist and tug her into me. "Missed me, huh?" I whisper against her lips huskily before I take them with mine.

After a searing kiss that makes my entire body as hard as my dick,

Lila moans and pulls back enough to breathe. I love when her cheeks flush like they are right now.

She traces my abs and the tattoo over my chest and stomach as she looks down. She's not smiling, and I don't like that at all. I run my fingers through her hair and tug slightly. Just enough so she looks at me. When her eyes meet mine, she looks like she's about to cry.

I furrow my brows and wrap my arms around her. "What's wrong, Lily?" It's something she only lets me call her. She tolerates her friend calling her Lily Pad, but I'm the only one who gets to call her Lily. Her favorite flower is a lily. She's even more beautiful than one.

Lila sniffles into my shoulder. "I just got a call from James," she whispers as she hugs me tighter.

I kiss her neck. "Do I have to kill him?" I tease, but I might be half serious. If they dropped her from the label or some bullshit, I might bring Hell to their doorstep.

She giggles, but I can still hear the sadness. "It's… good news… I'm just really apprehensive about it. And I had to give him an answer right away. I didn't think. I just said yes. But after I had the time to process…" She trails off.

I pull away just a little, but still hug her. Her grip on me tightens. "What happened, baby?"

She takes a deep breath. "Hayden Hart is on tour with Tate Matthews right now. They have four shows left. Hayden got super sick after their last show. He actually ended up being hospitalized. He's doing better, but they flew him home last night after he was released from the hospital. They need someone to open for Tate now…"

My heart beats a little faster. "And they asked you?"

She nods. "Mmhmm."

"I'm failing to see why you're crying, baby." I'm fucking ecstatic for her, but I don't know why she seems so upset.

She leans her head against my chest. I rest my chin on the top of her head. "I'm okay with the security the label gives for local tours… I feel safe, even though I'm getting those flowers and candy and the weird cards. They're doing well at dealing with it all. I'm even okay being without you because I know I'll be home during the week. And I have Leti and Dana with me so I don't feel lonely. But this is so different. I'm going overseas. The only people I know are Leti and Dana and the guys in my band. It's a huge arena show in a place I've never been so far away from the country I call home. I'm just a little scared."

"I see," I say as it all dawns on me. "Well, here's what we're gonna do." I nudge her head so she's looking back up at me. "We've been talking about having someone take over your private security that you trust. You know Jason said that one of his older brother's is looking to get out of LAPD. What if we offered him the job? And Jason said he'd be willing to fill in until it's all settled. We could have him travel with you."

She blinks a few times, but that light that shines in her eyes is slowly starting to make a comeback. "Really?"

"I'll call him right now. We can get the other stuff ironed out while we're traveling."

She bites her lip and gives me a hopeful smile. "We?" she asks softly.

I nod. "Yeah. We. I'm not letting you go on your own if you're scared, baby. I told you when this all started that I'd do all I could to support you. I'll talk to the Chief. James is my interim Captain. He'll take over the crew for the next shift, or however long we'll be gone. I have time off saved up anyway."

"Oh God, Blake! Thank you!" Lila hugs me hard. "Thank you! Thank you! Thank you!"

I hug her just as tight. "So, when do we leave?"

"About that…" Lila looks up at me with the most adorable guilty smile. "Two… hours…?"

"Christ, sweet girl." I lift her down from the counter and swat her ass. "Out. Go home and pack for us. I have phone calls to make. Meet me back here. We'll go as soon as I get shit taken care of."

She giggles and hurries out of the locker room. I groan when she teasingly shakes her ass at me and adjust myself. The effect she has on me is unlike anything I've ever experienced.

I hurry to get dressed, then rush to wake some people up. It's been an adjustment being the boyfriend of an up and coming celebrity, but I'm so proud of Lila, that I don't care what the challenges are that are thrown at us. Especially since I know it's my ring she wears on her finger.

I proposed six months to the day after we became an official couple. I took her out to our tree and had a whole special dinner and speech planned out. The words I'd practiced for hours, though, didn't come. I was too afraid that she'd tell me to fuck off; that I hadn't made all the years I'd screwed up better yet.

I barely got the words out, though, before she was kissing me and screaming yes. The next thing I knew, clothes were flying everywhere. We made love under that tree until the sun had long set. Thankfully, I've traveled to that tree in the dark many times and know my way.

Our engagement has been perfect. Lila has moved in with me. Murphey has replaced me with her. Even play wrestling gets a protective growl out of the fucker. Truthfully, though, I'm thankful for his protective instincts over her. The both of us, honestly. I know he has our back in the event anything happens.

I reach down and scratch behind his ears after I finish my phone calls. "What do you think? Ready for some fun with Uncle Luke?" I ask, looking down at him.

His head pops up, and he chuffs, shaking himself as he stands. He tilts his head.

"Yeah, yeah. Remind me why I love you again?"

He nudges my hand before jumping up on me.

I grin and pet him as he licks my face. "Well done. Good reminder. Let's go get Luke."

Murphey jumps down and bounds to the closed door. I open it for him. He takes off running in search of his uncle. I swear the dog understands every word that comes out of my mouth. When I reach him, he's getting a belly rub from his favorite uncle.

I chuckle. "Hey, Luke. I need a favor." I look up at everyone lounging in our den area with the TV playing low in the background. "Actually, everyone listen up. Something has come up, and I need to take a bit of time off."

Keelan's eyes snap up from his phone. "What's going on?"

"Did Lila talk to you?" I ask.

"Yeah, a little. She was in a hurry to get to you, but she told us she got an amazing opportunity opening for Tate Matthews."

I nod as I sit in my favorite leather lounge chair. "Yeah. She's covering for someone else for the last four shows of his tour. Starting in Glasgow and ending in London. She's excited about it, but also scared because it's her first time overseas without any of us. She trusts the security the label set up for her, but she would feel more comfortable with her own. People she knows. I got it all okayed with the Chief for me to take some time off to go with her, but James. I'll need you to play me for a shift or two."

"Not like you ever take time off. I got it covered," James says with a smile.

I nod. "Luke, I'll need you to take Murphey for me."

"No problem," Luke responds as he plays with Murphey.

I grin. "I didn't think it would be. Keelan, while we're gone, I need you to help me set up private security through Prestige Guardians. Jason is coming with and acting as her personal bodyguard, but we need something more permanent. We'll be working on the label to provide the fee they charge for her."

"Yeah. Good idea because even though I think Troy is a nice guy, he's expensive as hell," Keelan says as he goes back to his phone shaking his head.

He's not wrong. Prestige Guardians is one of the most elite protection firms in the nation. They provide security for celebrities right down to senators' families. And it was all started when Troy, one of Jason's three older brother's, got the idea of starting it up and providing security for people.

It began as Troy's baby. While in college, Jason helped out from time to time, but he's been immersing himself in it a lot more, even though he still runs and owns Papi's and Wiley's Cinema. Evan, the LAPD cop who wants to get out, is still a bit hesitant to join, but he knows there's always a place for him.

Troy never forgot their roots, though. They started small, providing security for those who couldn't afford a lot and needed to feel safe while their lives imploded. One of Troy's first cases was for a little boy who was testifying against his junkie father after he killed the boy's mother. That was in Wako, not too far from us. Wako police couldn't provide the type of security the little boy needed to feel safe. Troy did it at no charge.

Prestige Guardians was born, and took off. Now, while they still do those small scale jobs for the same zero dollar price, they caught the eye of some large scale clients. That price tag has gone up exponentially.

"You're telling me." I chuckle as I stand. "Okay. James, I finished everything that needs to be done, but I just heard Lila come in, which means I need to leave if we're going to catch the flight."

"Blake!" Jason yells from the bay. "Need to go, man! We got a private jet waiting, but we're on a tight schedule if she has a chance of getting there with any time to relax before she has to rehearse!"

"Thank God, y'all can sleep on the flight," Keelan says with a wink.

"Don't plan on sleeping," I say with a smirk.

"Asshole. Get out of here." Keelan throws a throw pillow at me. I catch it and drop it in the chair I just vacated before looking at James. "You good?"

"Not my first rodeo, Cap. We're good," he responds. "Get your girl to those shows."

I grin. "Keelan, can you get my gear home?"

"You got it."

"Thanks, man." I jog out of the den and to the bay where Jason is leaning against our ladder truck.

As soon as he sees me, he gives me a nod as he leads me out. "Troy is going to drive us to the airport. And then he's going to set up everything for her security with Keelan while we're gone."

"Good. I just told Keelan about it." I jump into the backseat of the truck where Lila is waiting. She smiles so brightly at me that my heart melts. I wrap an arm around her.

I feel her trembling with both nerves and excitement. I fully understand why. This is huge for her. She's bringing herself in front of a new audience opening for one of the biggest country acts in the world. She's already made a huge splash over the summer, but I feel like these three shows are going to catapult her to a level neither one of us are expecting.

Or ready for.

Chapter Thirteen

火 Lila 火

Somewhere over the Atlantic, I stir in Blake's arms. I don't have any idea how much longer we have until we reach Glasgow International Airport, but we were both exhausted enough to fall asleep almost as soon as we were in the air. Thank God the private plane has a small bedroom because it feels so nice to stretch out. I haven't been sleeping well if Blake isn't in bed with me, so when he's on shift, sleep is pretty much pointless.

I was awake when James called me about Hayden being off the tour. I was so excited about it that when he said he needed an answer right away so he could get my tickets, hotel, and my wardrobe ironed out as well as everything for the band, I jumped at saying yes. I never knew how much went into a show, even just an opening act, until I went on my summer tour.

It's crazy. The stage needs to be built. The lights all have to be rehearsed and programmed with a set list and things I don't even pretend to understand. I'm in awe of all of the people involved who are there to put the show on. All I have to do is get dressed, practice a little, and get up to sing. My job is easy.

Blake tightens his arms around me and groans. "I don't feel a descent. It's not time to move."

I can't help but giggle at the sexy raspiness in his sleepy voice. "So adorable when you wake up."

I can feel his smile against the sensitive skin against my neck.

"Adorable, huh?" His hand slides down my body as he pulls me closer so my butt is nestled more firmly into his dick.

When he reaches the waistband of my jeans, he flicks the button open and starts kissing my neck. I love the feel of him against me. Clothing or not, Blake is so hot. I love his tattoos, muscles, all of him. But one of my favorite things in the world is when he's shirtless and wearing jeans like he is right now. I love the way he looks in them. I love the worn belt he wears, and the silver buckle he uses with it. Mostly, though, I love when he pulls me against him, just like this, and holds me tight.

I love when he's touching me.

I shiver as he trails his fingers featherlight across the bare skin just underneath the button. "I'll show you adorable...," he rumbles as he nips and kisses my neck. His hand dives lower.

My eyes fly wide open when his long finger grazes over my already throbbing clit. "Oh..., Blake..."

He chuckles. "Promise to be a good girl and stay quiet?"

It's then that I remember there are other people on this plane, and that they can probably all hear everything that goes on in here. I nod. "I'm always your good girl."

"Mmm..., you are." He presses his hardening dick against my ass. I gasp. "Mmm..."

He slides one finger deep inside my already wet and waiting pussy and thrusts hard, deep, and slow. Every time he pushes in, he thrust against my backside, which makes his finger slide as deep as it possibly can. I'm already close to releasing, but when Blake sets his thumb against my clit and starts rubbing, the sensations shoot upwards and leave me breathless.

Blake's cocky smirk hits my skin again as he pushes another finger inside. My pussy clenches tighter than it already was. It pulses erratically. When he starts thrusting hard and deep again, I turn my face into the pillow to keep from crying out his name. I rock my hips into his hand as he drives me closer and closer to my peak. My thighs tremble. My stomach tightens. My pussy clamps down. I mumble incoherently into the pillow as I moan.

"Do you want to come, my little Miss America?"

"Blake, please...," I moan into the pillow as I buck wildly into him. I grip his wrist and grind myself into his fingers and thumb.

"Come for me, Lily...," he commands low, deep, and dominantly.

I scream into my pillow as silently as I can while my entire body shudders and jerks. My pussy convulses and spasms around him, and the entire time I'm coming, he's still thrusting. As I come down, he slows his thrusts more and more until my panting turns into more steady breathing.

"Not even close to being done with you and that pretty pussy of yours," he growls.

I smile as he removes his fingers from me. He gives me a sexy smirk as he sucks my taste off his fingers while he gets to his knees. He unzips my jeans and yanks them down with my panties. He throws them off.

I reach for the bulge his jeans are unable to hide, but that grin of his turns wicked as he pulls back. I pout and sit up as I look at him. "You *are* going to let me return the favor," I say with a spark of fire behind my words. "I want you in my mouth."

He grins as he straddles me. His fingers spear my hair and he tilts my head at just the right angle so I'm looking at him. "Completely judging from the time we left and the time it is now, we don't have time for you to suck my dick if I want to fuck you. Which I do. Against that wall." His eyes never leave mine, but he tilts his head towards the door to the bedroom and the wall next to it.

"There's no way you're fucking me there!" I whisper at him in shock. "There's only like a foot between the wall and the end of the bed. And you're way too tall! You'll hit your head…"

"Fuck that," he rumbles darkly with a grin capable of making me come again. "I want you all the time, baby. I can make anywhere work."

He tugs off my shirt as I laugh. Blake is so cocky, but he wears it so well. And it's a point in his favor that he's able to follow through with all of the things he says he can do. He does them with such ease. So, when my naked back hits the wall after he tosses my bra somewhere and then lifts me, I'm not at all surprised that he does just what he said and makes it work.

"My God, Blake…," I moan against his neck while I hold him tightly as he sinks his length deep inside me. He's perfect. He's thick and long. I've never measured him, but he's above average. There's no way he's below nine inches.

And he's all for me.

I dig my fingers into his back and hold on for dear life as he starts thrusting, deep, hard, and fast. I tighten my legs around him and meet him thrust for thrust. I use his shoulder and neck to muffle my moans and screams. I'm trying to be his good girl and stay as quiet as possible. I know how sweet the reward is if I follow his sexy rules. He always makes everything worthwhile.

I'm sure people can hear my back hitting the wall and our quiet panting. I'm so wet, they probably can hear Blake pumping into me. But all of it fades into the background when I'm in his arms; wrapped around him.

"Fuck, Lila...," Blake whispers sexily in my ear. I love his deep voice. "I love how wet you get for me. And how you're pretty pussy grips my cock like the good girl you are."

I blush. Shivers run down my spine. I bury my face further into his neck and grip as tightly as I can. My pussy pulses uncontrollably as it gets even wetter. I clench around him with each thrust he drills into me. He kisses my neck with a low, possessive rumble that makes the release that started as a gentle tingle roar into a raging inferno.

"Oh..., Blake...!" I whisper as my thighs tremble against him.

"Mmm..." The growl Blake releases is dangerous and dominant. It sends shockwaves of electricity erupting throughout my whole body as it spasms against him. They end in my core and make my pussy clamp so tight around him that it makes him gasp and moan. "Fuck..."

I can't speak. I can't make any noises other than moans; formulate words other than his name. I tighten my legs around his waist as my pussy pulses erratically around him. It only makes him thrust more wildly; harder.

I let my head fall back against the wall when he slams into me one last time... deep. He tangles his fingers in my hair and tugs lightly as he gives the command then kisses me deeply, sensing what is coming.

"Come, Lily. Come for me," he growls against my ear only loud enough for me to hear.

"Oh fuck! Yes! Blake!" I bite down on his shoulder to muffle my moans as my pussy clenches and spasms around him. I come hard, drenching us both as my hips jerk against his.

"Fuck, Lily," Blake moans into the kiss. I feel his dick throb inside me as he comes hard, jerking against my hips.

My pussy spasms around him as he fills me with jet after jet of him. I pant against his neck as I hold on for dear life. I can feel us both dripping down his dick, but it makes it so much sexier and dirty.

As we both come down, he starts sliding out of me. I hate when we lose that connection, but I can feel the plane losing altitude. It's a signal that we'll be landing soon. I giggle as we clean up and get dressed again, though he never actually lost his jeans. Just pulled them down enough to free his dick. When we finish, we head back to our seats.

Everyone wears their own brand of smirk, but luckily, no one says a word.

After we landed yesterday, I was almost instantly rushed to the O2 Academy in Glasgow. They gave us just enough time to eat something before heading to the venue. Got to love twenty-four hour McDonald's.

It's Thursday, and I'm just finishing up my rehearsal and sound check. I've already been fitted for the couple of outfits I'll be wearing. They're simple, but they need to be stage ready.

I never understood why some performers change clothing so often. I understand people like Taylor Swift or Britney Spears because their outfits go along with their entire production. For me, I don't have the whole big stage they do. I'm standing in front of a microphone. I'm not dancing around. I'm hyping the crowd and moving, but I don't do what they do.

But truth is, it has everything to do with how hot it gets up on that stage. The lights feel scorching sometimes, and it only takes a few songs before the clothing feels drenched and gross. Even if I'm just singing and playing to the crowd, my clothes feel like they're sticking to me. A cool down and clothing change is an incredible feeling. It may only be a few minutes, but it's enough to finish the set.

"I think you sound great, Lila!" James yells to the stage from where he's standing in the middle of the lower level. I can hardly see him, but it looks like he's walking towards me. "Tate needs to get up here and do his, but we're good with you. You can take off and rest up in the bus."

"Thanks, James!" I turn and hightail it off the stage. I'm so grateful to Tate and his team for being such gracious hosts to me. I don't want to upset anyone by taking his time up here. I haven't met him yet, but I'm sure he's as nice as everyone makes him out to be.

I hurry off the stage expecting to see Blake. I'm a little surprised when I see Jason standing there by himself and talking on the phone with his brows furrowed.

My heartbeat immediately quickens. I've already been sent a random set of flowers with another weird card. As usual, they didn't come from Blake or anyone I know. They've been being sent now ever since the very beginning of my summer tour. Everywhere I showed up, they were there.

I also found out recently that Daniel has been trying to get backstage to see me. Thankfully, he can't get through my security, but I'm starting to wonder if he's somehow keeping tabs on me and showing up wherever I am. I haven't talked to him. I refuse to, but it's getting a little unnerving. Especially thinking he might be the one behind the flowers with strange cards, and that he might be somewhere in the audience watching me.

It's like the *Bodyguard* plot. Only this isn't a movie. I'm not Whitney Houston. And this is real life.

"Yeah. I got it. It's okay. I'll be there to take care of it. In the meantime, just do what you can to make sure we reopen. If anyone needs my approval for anything, tell them to call me." He waits for a second as he starts to escort me away from the stage before he nods and hangs up. He looks down at me. "A storm hit last night. The roof of the theater collapsed. I was having it fixed this week because it had been leaking. I guess it didn't want to wait that long."

"Oh my gosh. I hope no one was hurt."

"No, it happened overnight after the cleaning crew left. No one got hurt, but the concession stand is wrecked. There's a lot of damage. Which means… I'm gonna have to take off. Evan is on his way out here, but Troy is going to have to finish the tour in London because Evan has to get back to finish his resignation time before he totally takes over your security."

My eyes widen hopefully. "I like Evan. He's going to be with me permanently?"

Jason nods. "He's given LAPD a thirty day notice. He's going to join Troy with the company. And it looks like I'm probably heading that way myself. At least part-time. For now."

I can't help but giggle. "Wasn't it you who always said your brothers were insane for doing what they do?"

Jason laughs. "Yeah. I did say that. But I've filled in a couple of times over the years. It's actually not that bad."

"Well, I hope you do what makes you happy. Whatever that might be. Where's Blake?"

"Oh. Forgot to tell you. He ended up going to lay down. I think coming straight here after his shift took a toll. He looked like he was about to pass out. He told me to tell you he loves you and is sorry for missing the rehearsal, but he wants to be awake and alert for the show. James has some food being set up in the bus for you. Light things. Not like burgers and fries."

I laugh. "I had enough McDonald's last night to last me awhile."

Jason grins as he opens my bus door for me. "James is going to do whatever it is he does. I'll be back here with him in a few hours. Get some rest. You could use it, too."

"Is Evan going to be here tonight?"

He shakes his head. "No. Troy sent him to the next venue to check things out. Evan said, and I'm quoting this, 'I'm going to make sure that girl has the fluffiest mattress in the world in that bus. And all the Twizzlers her heart desires. She'll be treated like the Town Princess she is.' He'll meet us there later on after the show. I'll fly home, and he'll take over the next two shows. Then Troy will meet you in London. I'm sorry I have to leave you like that."

"It's okay. I'm just glad you came for this one. You dropped everything. I'll never forget that or what anyone has done for me. I'm so grateful."

He hugs me. "Anytime, sweetheart. You deserve all of this. I'm so proud of you. We all are."

His words fill me with warmth and even more gratitude. He closes my door, and I smile when I see the spread of fruit, cheese, and some vegetables all sitting in a tray of ice on the small kitchen counter. There are also ice cold waters and a couple of sodas as well as iced coffee.

I check the time. I have a few hours before I need to be on stage for my set, so I take the opportunity to catch up on some sleep with the love of my life. As I crawl into bed with Blake, his arms automatically wrap around me. He pulls me close, but I'm convinced he's still dead asleep. I love how he instinctively knows I'm near him and cuddles me close.

I set my alarm to wake us up, but when it goes off, it doesn't seem like either of us slept long enough. I pout as sadly as possible as I shut it off. "It's going to take me forever to get onto this UK schedule."

Blake chuckles into my neck before he kisses it. "I think you'll do just fine. You're a tough girl. You kinda have to be to put up with my bullshit."

I laugh as we both get up and start to clean up. I change into my stage outfit that magically appeared in the bus while we were asleep. Simple stressed blue jeans that hug my curves and black cowboy boots to match my black tank top, but it's the belt that I'm so in love with. It's black leather, but the belt buckle is of a stallion rearing up, and it's pink. I was so happy when Keelan surprised me with it at my first show. Since that day, James has made sure that it goes where I do.

We quickly eat a little bit. I don't ever eat too much before a show, but I know I need the energy. And I'm obsessed with the iced coffee before I get on stage. It's something I always request. Lots of people have long lists of things that they require a venue to provide for them. I ask for Twizzlers and ice coffee. I've been told more than a few times that I'm the easiest celebrity they've ever dealt with.

Celebrity.

What a word. A word I can't seem to quite associate with myself. I just don't view myself as that.

Blake and Jason lead me from the bus to backstage. Tate is doing an autograph signing, so we pass a line of people happily waiting for their turn with him. No one pays me any mind, but I do hope they'll be seated by the time I get on stage.

After getting my makeup and hair touched up, and then equipped with my earpiece and battery pack, I'm ready for my set. I can hear an announcer on the stage talking to the crowd. People cheer.

Blake tugs me close and wraps me in his arms. "I love you," he says with a grin that sets any kind of fluttering butterflies I may have had at ease.

"I love you more," I whisper back.

He grins even wider. In true Blake fashion, though, he notices my hesitation. His grip tightens around me, and he hugs me tighter. "I know you're nervous. This is a huge venue with a lot more people in the stadium for an opening act. But you're so talented, baby. Everyone is so proud of you. I'm fucking ecstatic."

"I'm just nervous because they expect Hayden."

He shrugs. "But they're getting you. You're not below him. Just because they know him doesn't mean they aren't going to love you. Go out there. Show them just who the fuck you are and why they should love you. Get them hyped for Tate. Give them a show unlike anything they expect. Make them fall in love with you just as so many others are." He gives me a sweet kiss that fills me with the confidence he knows I need.

"We're ready for you, Lila," James says.

I nod and smile, stepping out of the comfort of Blake's arms. I follow James to the edge of the stage where I wait to be announced. Jason gives me a wink when I reach him. He'll be standing right here throughout my whole performance. The other security officers are at his command. That brings me so much comfort.

The crowd is buzzing; the cheers are deafening.

The energy of it all flows through me. Their cheers gets me more and more excited to start the show.

"Give it up for our newest act, Lila Rose!" the announcer says.

As I take my first steps onto the stage, only one thought runs through my mind…

Here we go…

Chapter Fourteen

 Blake

(Eight Days Later)

Down, down, down in flames
Not going easy
I'm taking you with me
Down, down, down in flames
There's no escape
You're no renegade
Down in flames

Down, down, down in flames
We're going down tonight
It'll be just right
Down, down, down in flames
Show you're attraction
Let me be your satisfaction
Down in flames

Down in flames
Down, down, down in flames

I watch my girl while I stand next to a beaming Troy. He leans into me. "I knew she was good, but damn. Look at her confidence in this show! And that song is fucking awesome live. I've only heard it on the radio."

I grin. "She's fucking amazing. People are singing the words to some of her songs, like this one. She wasn't sure people even knew who she was over here. But after that first night, she gained a lot of confidence. Tate Matthews spent a while talking to her before she went up for her rehearsal for the next show. Whatever he said to her made her feel good about this."

"Bet that boosted that confidence level through the roof!" Troy laughs.

I laugh. "He's talked with her a few times. James has a few collaborations in the works with some huge names."

"Shit, really?"

"She's royalty. She's been the Town Princess since the first time anyone heard her sing in public. No one is ever going to be able to take that title from her. The world is about to see what we've all kept hidden for so many years. She damn well deserves it all."

"Couldn't agree more."

I grin as Lila hypes everyone up for Tate. She skips across the stage as the crowd screams. It's hard to decipher who the screams are actually for because I can hear her name *and* Tate's being chanted.

She steps off the stage with the brightest smile I've ever seen. "Oh my God, Blake! Do you hear them?"

I wrap her in my arms. "I hear them, baby."

"We gotta go," Troy says as he starts to usher us both. "Tate's signing is wrapping up. I'd like to get her through before the VIP crowd gets released from their room to their seats for the show."

"Right." I reluctantly release her and let Troy do his job.

After the whirlwind of the first three shows, we got to do a little sightseeing with Dana and Leti. I've always wanted to do the Harry Potter walking and guided tour and was beyond ecstatic when James got us tickets. We got to see the Palace, Royal Albert Hall, and Tower of London. Lila really wanted to go to Madame Tussauds and the London Sea Life. We even went to the Tower of London and made out when we stopped at the top. It was a packed few days, but it was like a mini pre-honeymoon. We loved every second of it.

When we get back to the bus, James is standing outside grinning.

"Got your flight plan home."

Lila sinks into my side when I put my arm around her. "I honestly had the greatest time, but I'm ready to go."

"Well, I know you wanted to see the show tonight, so I have tickets to a private lounge for you. Anything you want, we'll take care of it. Drinks. Food. Whatever you need. From there, Tate and his team will be pulling out and heading home from Heathrow. We'll be flying out at the same time so security isn't split up. We should get into DFW noon London time. That would be six in the morning Dallas time. I have a driver lined up to drive the three of you back to Piper Falls and another to get the band Dana and Leti back." James looks at Troy. "Per your request, I spoke with Jason, and he vetted the drivers."

Troy gives him a grin and nod. "Just how me and my team works."

"Not as bad as some others. I appreciate the communication I get from your team." James gives him a curt nod before looking back at us. "I know this has been a whirlwind, Lila, but you did incredible. Word spread fast about you. Your merchandise booth sold out. The label is already planning a World Tour for next year."

Lila's eyes widen. "What? No."

James grins. "Yes. Now, get ready to go. We have a little less than an hour. Have your stuff ready so when he gets off the stage, we can get out of here."

Lila makes an adorable squeaking noise as she darts into the bus. I laugh and give both James and Troy a wink. "When do you need us for the show?"

"Thirty minutes. Gives us time to get to the lounge," James says.

I nod and step onto the bus, closing the door behind me. It doesn't take me long to figure out where my girl went. Judging by her squeals and squeaks, I know she's talking to Keelan about everything James just said. And I can pinpoint her to the bedroom.

I make my way back there and quickly pack the few things we have with us. It doesn't take long. When I finish, Lila is still talking to Keelan.

"I know! I still can't believe it. And they built me a website. James said yesterday that my merchandise is flying off the shelves there, too!" She squeals again.

I can't help my grin at her happiness. I'm happy for her, too, but she doesn't have a clue how sexy she looks when she's that excited. All I can think of right now is taking off those painted on jeans… with my teeth.

Fuck. Maybe I will.

I stalk towards her. When she catches my eyes, hers widen impossibly large and more adorable than they already are. She backs against the wall as I grin wolfishly and look her gorgeous body up and down.

"That's completely crazy to say," she says into the phone as she points to it and scolds me with her eyes. "Of course I'll still do the festivals at Walker Estate. I love Piper Falls."

I drop to my knees in front of her and grip her hips. I slowly move them to the belt buckle on her jeans and start to undo it.

"Blake!" she whispers as she holds the phone away from her. "What are you doing?"

I just give her a devilish smirk and pop the button on her jeans. I yank the zipper down a little roughly, but I know it will make her gasp.

Sure enough, she slaps a hand over her mouth to cover it as she holds her phone to her ear and watches me in shock. I lean forward and grip the waistband with my teeth. She whimpers almost silently while I drag the jeans with her panties down her legs.

"It was a contract provision. I still want to be doing things in my hometown that I've always done. And Piper Falls will still be home. I'm not moving away to some big city or something."

I tug her jeans and panties off the rest of the way when I get to her knee and drag my tongue up her thigh. She left her boots by the door when she came in. She loves them, but they've always been the first thing to come off when she wants to get comfortable. The second thing to go is usually her bra. If she's in for the night, that is. Not like I'm complaining. Her tits in my hands and mouth are among my most favorite things I've ever put into my mouth.

When I reach her pussy, I lick it, making her gasp and jump, before I go back to her other knee and start the tongue game all over again. Lila's quiet moans are getting a little louder, but she's still trying to hide them.

"Of course, Keelan. I wouldn't ever want to miss that," she says, gasping at the end as I lick her pussy. "I have to go, Keelan. See you soon! Love you!"

Lila throws her phone just as I dive into her pussy with my tongue. "Fuck, yes… Sweet. My favorite meal."

"Blake!" she gasps as she spears my hair with her fingers and tugs me closer.

She's already wet for me. And so fucking tight. She's dripping. I lap it all up, licking her relentlessly before diving back into her with my tongue. Her hips jerk over me as she arches against my mouth.

Her pussy spasms for me as she moans. I hold her against the wall and lift one of her legs over my shoulder so I'm at a better angle to bring her all of the pleasure she can handle. I nip and suck on her pussy before licking my way up to her clit. When I take it into my mouth and suck, she almost loses all control.

"Oh God, Blake!"

I growl against her clit knowing full well it's sending vibrations through her bundle of nerves and straight to her pussy. It causes her to scream out and buck over my tongue. I smile and lick her relentlessly from her clit and back down to her pussy. I thrust my tongue into her hard and flick it against the spot inside her that I know drives her crazy.

Words suddenly start eluding her, and she begins speaking in moans, groans, and whimpers. Her pussy pulses around my tongue and clamps down. I grin and start sucking as I set my thumb against her clit. She doesn't need the extra pressure, but I love when she comes hard for me.

"Oh…"

"Fuck, Lila. Come, baby. Come all over my tongue like the good girl you are…," I rumble the command.

"Ah! Blake!" she screams, slapping a hand over her mouth to try and muffle it. Her pussy pulses erratically as she trembles against me. She slides her pussy over my tongue. I rub her clit faster as I thrust my tongue as deeply and quickly as I can.

Just like I wanted, she comes for me, hard, soaking my tongue in all of her sweetness. I moan against her and lick it all. Her body convulses until she nearly collapses. I grin and kiss her pussy as I hold her against the wall.

"I think you have just enough time for a shower before we need to get out of here," I say as I stand. I wrap her in my arms and hold her close as she regains the strength she lost with her powerful orgasm.

After a few moments of hugging me, she tilts her chin up and kisses me long and deeply. She sucks on my tongue. I know she can taste herself on me, and she may never admit it, but I know she likes it, and it turns me on even more for my girl.

She pulls away slowly. "I don't think I have enough time for a shower."

"You're probably right. We only have about fifteen minutes, but that's enough time to clean up. I'll grab you some clean clothes. I left a change out for you."

She smiles and nuzzles my jaw before hurrying to the small bathroom on the bus. I smile and turn to her suitcase where I left the change of clothes. I catch a glimpse of my phone and see a text, so I pick it up to read it.

Keelan: Fucking asshole. You think I haven't been around long enough that I wouldn't recognize those noises? I'm gonna kick your ass when you're stateside.

I can't help but laugh as I type out my response.

Me: You haven't been able to kick my ass since I was fourteen. But sure. Whatever you say, sunshine.

I laugh at his response of a middle finger emoji and slide my phone into my pocket. I grab Lila's stage outfit and fold it for James. I don't know what he does with it, but I assume it goes with her wardrobe stuff.

Hours later, after the show when we're in the air and on our way home, Lila sleeps soundly curled into my side. She exhausted us both by insatiably sucking my dick like her very own lollipop and then riding me until we both collapsed. I shift just enough to wrap her in my arms and bury my face in her sweet smelling hair.

In just a month, Lila is going to meet me at the altar.

And I can't wait until she officially becomes Lila Rose Falcon.

Chapter Fifteen

 Lila

(One Week Later)

"Ugh!" I yell as I throw my purse on the floor. I sit down on the bench next to the door and put my shoes on.

Blake is amazing. I love him more than anything. While we were in the UK, he made plans to put in an amazing recording studio for me in the basement of his house. Well, our house, which is something he's made perfectly clear since the day I moved in. The studio is going to be amazing, and I'm truly so excited for it.

But I hadn't really thought it would be this noisy.

Drilling.

Banging.

Yelling.

Sawing.

And oh my God, the awful Polka music! Who, other than grandparents, listens to Polka music and actually likes it? It's wrong.

I take out my phone and text Blake.

Lila: Hi, sexiest fire Captain. I'm heading out. I love you, but the assholes downstairs are driving me insane. If I don't leave the house, I'm breaking up with you.

I start to tie my laces then think better of shoes and put on flip flops. I'm probably going to have to change when I get to where I'm going.

I pick up my phone when it dings and smile when I see Blake's name.

Blake: Are they playing Polka music again?

Lila: Ha! The Polka music doesn't stop. I hear it in my sleep. I know it will be worth it, but right now, I'm going to go mad.

I pick up my purse and start to open the door. I scream when it's pushed open and quickly duck when someone comes in carrying several two-by-fours.

"Sorry, ma'am," one of the young workers drawls with wide eyes. His shirt is dripping sweat, even though the day has just begun, and I have to fight to keep from gagging at the overpowering smell of body odor.

I shake my head. "It's fine." I duck underneath the boards and hurry out the door.

"Hey! Would you watch what you're doing? Christ!" an older guy barks at the young guy. "Don't take off without someone on the end of these. We don't want to break anyone's property!"

"Sorry, sir," the young guy says as the guy grabs the end of the boards.

I stay out of the way as they make their way inside and look down at my phone again when it goes off.

Blake: Well, you have that photoshoot and you're trying on dresses today, right? You'll be okay, baby. You're getting out for a while.

Lila: It's a good thing. I almost packed my stuff.

I smile. One of my favorite things to do is joke around with Blake. I love that he not only gives it right back to me, but he also knows I'm kidding around and doesn't take me seriously. I don't think I can be in a relationship where I can't kid around. Daniel never liked humor or anything. I question myself constantly on how I thought I could settle for a man like him. I had to have been crazy.

Blake: Ha! Yeah, right. You love my cock too much.

I giggle because he's very much correct with that statement. It's not the only reason I'm with him, though.

Lila: Excuse you. I happen to love your personality, dominance, adorableness, sexiness, voice, eyes, height, protectiveness, how hot you are in a uniform, how annoying you are when you attempt to sing, and most importantly... the way you love me.

Blake: Well, now you're just making me blush, baby girl. And getting me hard in front of the assholes I work with. How 'bout you get your ass down here and do something about that? Get you out of the house.

Lila: Well, see, I'd really love to... But I have this crazy thing called a photoshoot. I know, I know. But you can think of how wet I am right now thinking of you pounding me while I'm bent over your desk.

Blake: Fuck, Lila. Stop that. We just got a call. You want me sporting a hard on in front of the good people of Piper Falls?

I laugh out loud.

Lila: Go to work, Captain. I'll text you later. And maybe send you a dirty pic or two.

Blake: Ha! Do that. Please. Get me through the damn night.

Lila: Yes, sir.

I giggle and put my phone away as Evan pulls up in his truck. I know what calling Blake 'sir' does to him. If he wasn't sporting an impressive hard on before, he certainly is now. I hurry to Evan's truck and jump in as someone else is getting out. I raise an eyebrow at him as the stranger closes the door for me.

"He's staying here while you're gone. I'm not trusting anyone to be in that house alone without you or Blake there. Ready to get out of here?" he asks with his patented smirk as he nods to the house.

"So ready. I was almost decapitated by two-by-fours on the way out. They're still playing Polka music. And I might actually end up strangling someone. How come I didn't have someone here when Blake left this morning?"

"Good question. And the answer is because I was going to be here not long afterwards. Not only that, but I know you lock the door to your bedroom after Blake leaves."

I smile. "I do."

"And they all just got here a few minutes ago."

I roll my eyes. "Yeah. And already with the Polka music."

Evan laughs and nods to his cup holder. "Coffee."

My eyes widen, and I take it eagerly. "Oh God, thank you." I close my eyes as I take a sip and melt. "Yep. This is what I needed."

"Just buttering you up for the news I have about Daniel."

My eyes snap open. I growl low and glare out the window, keeping my coffee to my face. "What about him?"

"Still can't prove shit about the flowers and everything. It would've been great if he sent a card or something with them. I have nothing right now."

I sigh. "He might be dumb as bricks in love, but he really is smart in other areas."

"Well, I have a couple of leads. I'm not giving up."

I smile. "I really didn't think you would. You're a bloodhound."

"Why thank ya, ma'am," he drawls.

I laugh. "I'm kind of excited about this shoot. My first album cover!"

"It's gonna be pretty ep-" Evan's arm suddenly flies directly into my chest as my eyes widen. "Brace!" he yells.

I scream and drop my iced coffee. It splatters all over me, but I don't care. I brace with both hands on the roof of the truck just like Blake taught me to do if I was ever in an accident. Other than wearing a seatbelt, it's one of the safest things a person can do beyond covering their face and head to avoid impact as best as they can. I close my eyes as Evan jerks the wheel.

"Ah!" I scream again when I feel something hit us. It sends us spinning.

Glass shatters around us.

Metal crunches and scrapes against other metal.

"Ah!" More glass rains around me as I feel us hit by something once more.

I try to brace myself the best I can, but we're spinning the other way now. My body flails at the sudden change of direction. I hit my head against something and instantly feel myself going dizzy.

"Lila!" Evan screams.

With shaky arms, I cover my head in an effort to avoid any more hits and protect myself from the glass I feel flying everywhere.

I keep my eyes closed, but the blackness I was seeing behind my eyelids begins turning white and gets fuzzy. Gold stars start bursting in front of me.

I feel like I'm going to be sick. My stomach is rising up my throat. I don't know if I should fight that or fight passing out.

It doesn't matter much anyway. My body makes the decision for me. I don't have a chance. I feel myself slipping deeper and deeper. I feel the glass piercing my skin, but I don't feel the pain I should.

Instead, I'm lulled into a deep sleep…

Chapter Sixteen

火 Blake 火

I'm still smiling over mine and Lila's text exchange while I'm going over reports when I hear the alarm bell start going off signaling a call. I lock the computer screen and sprint out of my office.

I listen as our dispatcher's voice comes over our speaker to tell us the call details. "Hit and run on Silver Way, half-mile from Alcove Road. Truck with two occupants flipped upside down."

"Shit," Keelan says when I reach the bay area. I start quickly throwing on my gear as I nod.

"Male occupant is conscious and alert. He reports no injuries but a few abrasions he says are caused by glass. Female is unconscious. Unresponsive. Caller says she also has several abrasions and is bleeding from her right temple, but she is breathing."

I finish pulling up my fire retardant pants as I listen and grab my fire proof jacket. I'm the second person into the truck, just behind Luke, and just in front of Keelan and everyone else.

"Both occupants are trapped in the vehicle. Smell of gasoline. Caller says he can't get out. They're suspended upside down. Medical has been dispatched."

"Fuck," I growl as I snap my radio's mic to my jacket. "49 is en route," I say when I key the mic. Luke starts driving out of the bay as I flip on the lights and sirens.

"10-4," the dispatcher says.

"Luke," I call over the sirens as I turn to him. "When we get there, take Ashe. Grab the extinguishers."

"Yes, sir," Luke rumbles as he navigates the streets towards the scene of the crash. I'm just about to bark out more orders when I'm interrupted once more by our dispatcher's calm voice. She's been with us for a while and really has a knack for staying calm. A much needed quality for someone in her position.

"49, PD just arrived. Heavy smell of gasoline. Officers say it's leaking on the ground. Smoke is coming from under the hood of the car, but they can't open it to vent it."

"Oh, fuck," Ashe says.

I hold up a hand as I key the mic once more. "Tell them to assess and report. We're a couple minutes out." I grip the hand rest on the door as Luke makes a turn. "Make sure that car is stable."

"10-4"

"I don't like the sound of this, Cap!" James calls from the back. "Smoke from under that hood can be any number of things! Add the fuel on top of that? We could come up on a huge problem."

Unfortunately, I know that too well. I nod and turn back to my crew. "Keelan and James on the hose. Go in through the air vent in the front to douse those flames. They may not see them, but they're there. I'll take PD and medical and work on getting the driver and passenger out. We need that vehicle as stable as possible, as quickly as possible."

"Uh, Blake?" Luke says.

I can hear the panic in his voice, and it causes me to whip around quickly. His eyes are wide, and he's pointing out the window. I follow his gaze and see nothing but chaos. The accident wasn't far away from our headquarters so it doesn't take long to get there. There are two squad cars blocking both sides of the accident so no traffic can get through. There are skid marks from squealing tires on the asphalt. Glass and parts of the truck are scattered all over the road.

But that's not what has my attention.

It's the smashed up truck settled on its roof that has my mouth dropping and my heart kicking up to a supersonic speed that's completely unnatural.

"Fuck... Lila!" I start to jump out of the rig before Luke is totally stopped, but Keelan grabs me.

"Blake! Fucking stop! Let him park!"

I gasp for air as I watch the truck for any signs that an explosion could happen. I know fuck well it could, but observing forces my mind to calm while my team does what they need to do. I see one of the officers kneeling next to the driver's side window. He glances over his shoulder, and I can see it's Lieutenant Caden Andrews, Evan's brother.

"Shit. Oh, shit," I jump out as soon as Luke stops.

Like a well-oiled machine, everyone springs into action. We secure our rig with a block to keep it from moving. Not that it would. It's a precaution and one way we make the scene as safe as possible. It takes seconds, but it's seconds too long. I need to check on my girl. I'm battling between being a Captain and a boyfriend, but as Luke, me, and Ashe run towards the overturned truck, boyfriend wins.

Trusting my team, I beeline directly for Lila. I drop next to the passenger side window. "Baby?"

I shakily look her over. Her seatbelt is holding her securely in place. She's scratched up from the glass, but it's only on her arms. It looks like her face is okay. I see no cuts on her chest or neck. She has blood on the right side of her face and in her hair, but I can see clearly it's from a gash on her temple.

"He fucking came out of nowhere, Blake," Evan says. "I know it was fucking Daniel. I hope my dashcam got everything."

I glance at him as I'm checking for a pulse on my girl. "You saw him?" Miraculously, I keep my voice even. Lila is breathing.

"I saw the driver coming at us, and I'm sure, but we need the proof," Evan says.

"Cap! We need to get them out right now!" James yells.

"I haven't moved them. I had orders to wait for medical," Caden says, making eye contact with me.

I don't even have to look. I know the situation has changed drastically just by the smoke I see starting to billow out from the dash. I can hear the crackling that's quickly turning into a dull roar. I know something ignited the gas. Whether it's the line or the tank is what matters.

I look at Caden. "Cut them out. Try to keep them as steady as possible. We don't want to cause any injury to their neck or spine if we can help it."

"My legs are trapped, Blake," Evan says.

"Cap! Time to move!" Luke yells as he drops next to me with a backboard.

I take a second to look over the scene and see quickly that he's right. Keelan drops next to Caden and quickly gets to his hands and knees to look at how trapped Evan is. I take out my knife and waste no time cutting Lila's seatbelt as Luke steadies her so she doesn't fall when she's released. At least so she doesn't fall hard.

"Got her?" I ask before I make my last cut.

"Got her," Luke assures me.

"Cap! Get them out of there!" James yells. "Ashe! Get that foam on the line! Now! Move it! It's going to reach the tank!"

"Oh fuck!" Keelan says with wide eyes as he holds Evan while Caden makes his cuts.

Lila drops into Lukes arms, and we both drag her out of the truck. We put her on the backboard just as the ambulance shows up.

"No time!" Luke yells as I grab a strap to strap her down and secure her. "Get her back! I'll help Keelan!" He jumps up and rushes to help Keelan.

Ashe is spraying foam on the truck to douse the flames. James is doing all he can to keep the fire in the front at bay, but there's not a lot he can do. There's no possible way to get the hood open without tools. It's too damaged. The priority is to save Lila's and Evan's lives.

I keep Lila on the backboard and drag it with her as I pull her away from the car. It's not what I want to do. It's not near what I want to do. I want to pick her up and cradle her, but I know enough to know that she could be injured. Moving her too much could cause complete paralysis.

I get her back to the paramedics and watch as Keelan, Luke, and Caden pull Evan from the wreck. The front of the truck, despite the water being sprayed on it, is in worse shape than it was when we got here. Flames are starting to shoot out from the cracks, but it's the undercarriage of the truck that has me worried. I'm used to how quickly things change, but fuck am I glad getting her out wasn't that hard because even though Ashe is working to douse the flames, the fuel tank is dangerously close to exploding.

"Get on that tank!" I call over to them as Keelan and Caden reach me with Evan.

James does as I say without question as Luke runs back to help with another extinguisher he grabbed from our rig. James goes back to spraying the front of the truck. The paramedics work on Lila. Evan is talking to his brother about what happened.

"Cap, we need to get her to the hospital," one of the paramedics says. "She'll be okay, but we need to get her to a doctor."

I nod as I look at a shaky Keelan. He meets my eyes. As much as I want to go with them to be with my wife, I know I have to stay here.

"Blake...?" he asks with tears in his eyes.

I look down at Lila as they strap her to a gurney. I take a breath, lean down and kiss her softly, and nod again as I look back at Keelan. "Go. Go with her. Take Evan. I'm sure Jason and Troy will be down there soon."

Keelan nods and takes off after the paramedics as they load Lila. Evan nods to Caden and follows. I let out a breath when the guys get the fire under control.

"I hope I'm able to get some paint or some shit off his truck," Caden says to me. "It's fucking hard to get evidence off a car that's on fire."

"The fuel line looks like it's put out." I glance at the tow truck as it comes to a stop next to one of the squads. The more I look over the scene, the more pissed off I become. "We need to get those flames under the hood out. I don't want evidence burned away."

"I grabbed his dashcam after we got him out."

I nod as Luke runs back to the truck to grab supplies. As if he's thinking along the same lines as me, which doesn't surprise me at all, he pulls out tools. With the assurance that Lila is going to be okay and Evan is good, I jog over to help Luke with one thing and one thing only on my mind.

Once I meet Daniel face to face... I'm ripping him to shreds.

Chapter Seventeen

 Lila

(Three Weeks Later)

The day has finally come. Walker Estate is filled with people, as it usually is on Halloween. Blake and I are on a separate part of the ranch, though, and the people in this private section are here just for us.

Despite the bruises and scratches from the accident, I feel amazing. There's barely a physical reminder of that day. And while we still don't know who hit us, we still have our suspicions. It's just a matter of proving it. Without evidence, it's my bodyguard's word over Daniel's, and we all know he'll lie. Caden, Evan, and Troy are all working overtime to create an iron tight case against him.

"It's crazy out there," Dana says as she adjusts my black veil over my hair and down my back.

I smile brightly at her in the mirror as I look myself over. "I know. I'm so excited to finally be marrying Blake. I've dreamt about this forever."

The girls squeal a little as they continue getting ready. I smooth my dress down and make sure everything is in place. I'm not one to primp, but today is different. My silk, form fitting, strapless black dress flows down my body and moves like a second skin. Even with my black cowboy boots that give me an inch or two of height, the dress just brushes the ground.

The black veil isn't meant to go over my face. It's meant to flow down my back. It reaches the ground, too, and looks like a spider web. My long hair is down, but there are two pieces on the side that are braided. They meet in the middle of the back of my head and are braided together. I have silver rhinestones in my hair to make me shine and make the web look shimmery. Blue Baby Bells and Baby's Breath are interwoven throughout the braid, giving the illusion I'm wearing a crown of flowers.

My makeup is understated and subtle, as it always is, but I'm wearing body glitter so it looks a little like I'm a spider web. Everyone thought I was totally insane for wearing black on my wedding day. Faye told me she thinks it's bad luck. But Halloween is one of my favorite times of year. I couldn't allow it to go by without having a little bit of fun. Especially with Blake being totally onboard with the idea.

I wonder what people thought when we told them to come dressed up in costume. I haven't seen anyone yet, but if they look anything like the four girls in this room with me, I think we're going to have a blast. Who doesn't love a Halloween themed wedding?

I look up at the knock on the door. It's nearly time to walk down the aisle of lilies to the love of my life. I turn when my dad comes in with a huge smile. He's still a tall man and muscular, though he's nearing sixty. His once brown hair is now more salt and pepper, but his eyes are the same mischievous hazel of Keelan's.

Leti, Dana, Faye, and Adalle all giggle as they leave the room. My dad closes the door behind them and smiles widely at me as he walks slowly towards me. His eyes take all of me in, and I see the slightest hint of a tear. I've never seen my daddy cry.

He holds out his hands. I take them. He twirls me in a slow circle. When my eyes meet his again, his grin has spread across his whole face. His eyes crinkle at the sides. "You make a beautiful bride. I always knew you would. Your mom always thought you'd wear white, but I knew better. Not our girl. You've always wanted to do things your own way."

I blush. "Thank you, daddy."

He squeezes my hands. "We got a good day. Rain held off, and it's not so hot."

"Thankfully, we have a large tent set up for the reception. With the portable kitchen. I can't even begin to tell you how hungry I am. I can already smell the beef brisket and corn."

Dad laughs. "You should see the size of the T-bones they're

serving. Blake and I were both salivating."

I giggle. "It'll be a true Texas feast. Lamb. Chicken fried steak. Duck!"

Dad laughs again. "Well, we need to get through the vows first. What'd'ya say to making an honest man out of Captain Blake Falcon?"

My smile brightens. "Yes, please. I'm so excited for this day. It's all I've wanted for almost my whole life."

"I remember you following your brother and his friends around. I thought you were just smitten with being like your big brother. Who knew my little girl had a crush that she'd never get over?"

I blush. "Blake always made me feel like he didn't mind teaching me new things. I guess I didn't really think too much about anything more than that at first. I just thought it was cool to learn all these grown-up things. But then I realized it was a crush. Who knew that when I got older he'd start to see me as more than his best friend's annoying little sister?"

"I'm glad the two of you finally realized that you were meant for each other. We all thought that when you turned eighteen Blake might make a move and talk to you, or you to him. Or that one of you would talk to Keelan. But you both are so stubborn." Dad lets go of one of my hands and tucks some hair behind my ear. "All I know is we're all happy this is finally happening. I think I might have refused to give you away to Daniel if he'd ended up proposing."

I wrinkle my nose. "God, I can't believe how much I found out about him. The waitress at Aurora Heights. His secretary. And then so many bar chicks. Ugh. I'm so disgusted. I really wish he'd just leave town."

"As long as he stays away from my little girl, he'll be okay here."

I laugh. My dad is a kind, well-respected man, but don't mess with his little girl. The man has a shotgun, a shovel, and a place to bury a body all picked out. "I love you, dad."

"Love you, too, my girl. Now, let's get you married."

I squeak and squeal as I jump up and down. "Yes!"

He grins and leads me out of the cooled tent my team set up for me. Jaxon got a kick out of all of the people who showed up to set up for this. We're away from the festival he has going on for the kids, but it's still his property. He offered to do all of this, but I just wanted him to be a guest on our special day. He does so much for this town. He deserves a day to just kick back and relax.

Dad leads me down a closed off path that blocks me from everyone's view. I know my team has allowed a few photographers into the ceremony. I know Evan has a whole team around here to maintain order and security so no ruins mine and Blake's day.

When we make it to where I'll be exiting and revealing myself, the bridal party has already started to walk down the aisle. Jason escorts Adalle. Luke escorts Leti. Keelan escorts Faye. Last, Blake's brother, Elden, the best man, escorts Dana, my maid of honor.

I lean down and make sure the pillow that holds our wedding rings is securely fastened to Murphey's torso. I nuzzle his nose and kiss his snout.

"Go find, daddy," I whisper.

His ears perk up. He nuzzles me back as I hug him, then trots down the aisle towards Blake to calls of 'ooh,' 'awe,' and 'good boy.'

I wish I could see how adorable it is, but that's why we have so many photographers and videographers. I'll be able to relive this day every day of my life with Blake.

Finally, it's my turn.

The tent doors had been tied open, but I was back far enough that I couldn't be seen. When I finally step into everyone's line of sight, I hear sniffles and gasps. The decorations are perfect. There are hay bales lining the edge of the tent with pumpkins on top. The seating are all hay bales with orange cushions on top of them so people don't get poked in the butt when they sit.

Hanging from the poles at the top of the tent are halloween-esque decorations, like sparkly pumpkins, shimmery webs, and glittering spiders. There are orange and white fairy lights twined around the poles, and a couple of lanterns hanging from the top poles of the tent with the decorations. They're battery operated, per Blake's request. Less risk of a fire hazard.

Everyone is dressed in costume, including the staff, and my heart melts at all of the small details that James made sure to take care of that I would have never thought about. Even the photographers, who are very respectful in snapping their photos, are dressed up.

I tighten my grip on my dad's arm as he walks with me down the aisle. My feet brush over the soft orange and black petals under my feet. I grip my bouquet of white lilies a little more, not out of nerves, but because of the beautiful man who is standing at the altar waiting for me.

Each of the bridesmaids are wearing a black dress with spaghetti straps and an orange sash around their waist. Each of the groomsmen are wearing black slacks, cowboy boots, and a black dress shirt with an orange tie. Even Murphey is wearing an adorable tuxedo vest.

But it's Blake my eyes are on and have never left. He's wearing the same clothing as his groomsmen. Nothing is different. But he's the one who stands out to me. Maybe it's his smile. Maybe it's the fact that he seems larger than life. Or maybe it's the fact that his eyes are only on me, and like mine, tears of joy shine in them.

I've written many songs about Blake. Everything from imagining my life with him and what our love would be like, to how realistically heartbreaking everything was.

It all pales in comparison to our real love song.

As the officiant asks who gives me to Blake and my dad answers, I'm lost in Blake's gentle touch when he takes my hand in his. The words that come out of the officiant's mouth uniting us as husband and wife sink in, but the only thing that matters to me is Blake.

His eyes.

His smile.

His thumb rubbing soothingly back and forth across the back of my hand.

The entire world falls away. It's just me and Blake.

When the officiant announces us as husband and wife, Blake wastes no time sweeping me into his arms and kissing me as he holds me bridal style. I wrap my arms around his shoulders as I melt into the kiss as I giggle. He's already running up the aisle with me in his arms.

I hold him tighter as he carries me wherever it is he's taking me. I'll go wherever he wants me to. I'll follow him anywhere.

I'm finally Mrs. Lila Rose Falcon.

Chapter Eighteen

☖ Blake ☖

(One Month Later)

My eyes snap open. My stomach tightens, but I'm not quite oriented enough to figure out why. I look around the room. The sun is just coming up, so the room is just starting to brighten.

I feel something wet licking my dick. My first thought is that it's Murphey, but he's sleeping happily in the dog bed Lila bought him, and the wetness I feel isn't that of a rough tongue. It's soft and velvety.

"Oh fuck...," I rumble as my eyes roll back in my head. I manage to look down just long enough to see my wife's head bobbing up and down as she takes me into her mouth. "Fuck, Lila." I tangle my fingers in her hair and let my head fall back against the pillow.

She giggles and moans as she sucks hard and fast. The vibrations from her moans shoots straight through my tip all the way to my balls. She has them tightening in seconds.

"Mmm..." she moans again. I jerk. Her tongue twirls around my cock as she takes me as far into her mouth as she can. Every time I touch the back of her throat, she swallows.

"Fuck, baby." I start thrusting into her mouth because I can't stop myself.

She stops bobbing her head and lets me guide her. I hold her head still while I fuck her mouth. She keeps sucking and swallowing around me

132

until that familiar sensation jolts down my spine. I have no chance to warn her before my dick thickens, and I'm shooting jets of come down her throat.

"Mmm..." She swallows everything I give her and licks the rest of what dripped out of her pretty mouth off me.

"Oh God, baby girl."

She licks her lips as she sits up on her knees. "It's Thanksgiving Day."

I grin. "Mmhmm."

"We need to get Crew B their dinner. We have to prepare so much stuff. We're not going to have it done in time if we don't start now." She giggles as she jumps out of bed and starts throwing on clothes.

I laugh. "So, this is why you just sucked my dick. You want me to start slave labor right now. I see how it is. Finally get over myself and marry you only to end up taking orders from you, becoming your slave, and getting paid with nothing but sex."

She looks over her shoulder as she bends, giving the perfect view of her pussy. "It's good sex, though." She pulls up her jeans, wiggling her ass.

I throw the covers off my legs and dart out of the bed. She squeals and laughs, dodging me. "This isn't over, brat!" I call after her as she runs out of the bedroom door laughing.

"I hadn't planned for it to be!"

I laugh because of course it's part of her scheme. Ever since we got together, she's been coming up with different plots to get me into bed. Not like I mind in the slightest. One of my favorite places in the world is inside her.

I quickly shower and get dressed. When I get downstairs, Lila already has a cup of coffee and a bowl of mixed fruit waiting for me.

I raise an eyebrow. "Not that I'm complaining because you know I love and appreciate everything you do for me, but this seems kinda light."

"I thought since we'll be pigging out in a few hours, this would at least give you the energy you need to help me get everything prepared."

I grin and look her up and down. "I can think of a lot more tasty things to give me this energy you speak of." In a flash, I'm behind the counter, pinning her between it and me as I pepper her neck in kisses while I grind my dick into her ass.

"Ah! Blake!" Lila squeaks as she laughs and giggles.

I smile as I pull away and slap her ass. "Alright, boss. What do you need from me?"

Lila gives me an adoring smile that makes me wish I didn't have the level of control I do. I could have her jeans down and be pounding her pussy from behind right now. Self-control. My fucking blessing and curse.

"So, we can get all of this stuff prepared and going. I need the turkey for Crew B in the fryer. We have to get them their stuff before everyone else gets here. I want to make sure they're fed since they work today. But it only takes an hour, so you can help with everything else before we do that."

I lean against the counter and smile down at my girl. I've always been attracted to how sweet she is, but the older we've gotten, the bigger her heart has gotten. She wants to make sure the firefighters on duty today are getting to eat good food.

The truth is, we've always had a volunteer go in and cook the meal for the team working. If they got a callout, they don't have to worry about having to turn things off and ending up with a ruined meal. That's the incredible thing about living in a small-town where everyone is so close-knit. Someone does the same thing for the police department every year. No one, working or not, goes without on any of the holidays around here.

I lean down and kiss the top of her head. "Yes ma'am," I drawl.

I watch her visibly shiver and return my smile. I help her cut up potatoes and everything and get them all cooking.

After all of that, I open the fridge and take out one of the three turkeys we bought. We had to clear out a bunch of space in our refrigerator to get them in there. I thought Lila was going to be upset at the amount of work we'd be doing today, but she's taken all of it in stride. We did what we could last night to ease the strain, but we still have plenty to do today.

I put the turkey on the counter, then head outside to get everything ready for the turkey frying. I set a table up in the garage for myself to prep the turkey while the oil in the fryer is heating up. I won't leave it unattended. Way too large of a chance of it starting a fire.

After setting up the fryer with the oil, I head back into the house to grab the turkey. Lila is elbow deep in potato peeling. I can't help but laugh because it looks like a tornado went through the kitchen. I was only outside for five minutes.

"Baby, take that stuff outside. I set a table up. I'll peel and cut while the turkey is down. You can clean up in here and get the pie going."

She smiles brightly at me. "Thank you."

I give her a quick peck on the lips as I head back outside with the turkey. I turn the fryer on to heat the oil before I work on injecting the turkey with a specially made, flavorful injection, and then rub the turkey down with dry rub. By the time I'm done prepping the turkey, Lila has an assembly line set up going on the table with all of the vegetables. I carefully get the turkey down in the oil and then sit down to start the work she's set up for me.

Not that my mind isn't on several other ways to pass the time. Like how good she'd look pressed against my truck while I fill her pussy.

When I finish, I bring everything to the kitchen while keeping a close eye on the turkey through the window. Lila is making pies. I kiss her with a grin at how adorable and happy she looks.

On my way back out, I see Evan's truck pull into my driveway. I raise an eyebrow and look at my watch as he steps out. "You're a little early."

He grins. "I'm so fucking early. But this can't wait."

I lean against the frame of the garage and fold my arms over my chest, crossing my left foot over my right. "Is this about to ruin my day?"

"Nope." He grins. "I know we had our suspicions on who was sending Lila the flowers and candy and cards and all the bullshit, but it just got confirmed. I had my brother run a few things for me. It's fucking Daniel."

"No shock here. How'd you find out?"

"Fucker used a fake name on his credit card. We just traced that fake name to someone who works within his company. Only there is no such person. He gave a false name, but created an entire damn identity. Social security number and everything."

I shake my head. "How?"

Evan shrugs. "Black market. You can get anything through it. Digital copies of books, music, movies, real livers, hearts, and kidneys, a lamborghini. And yes, even a brand new, shiny identity."

"How the fuck do you even get connected with shit like that?"

"There are criminals all over the place, Blake. One thing I learned from being a cop. Hell, for all we know, that new girl who bought the cabin just North of the town and started working at Papi's is a drug lord or some bullshit."

I shoot him a glare. "Don't fucking talk like that, asshole. We don't need that shit in our town. I deal with enough without drugs being poured into the damn town."

He laughs. "Not saying she is. Just sayin' she's a sweet girl, but sometimes the sweetest ones have the darkest history."

"I get what you're saying. What are we doing with Daniel?"

"Caden took a few other cops and is arresting him as we speak. Fraud and several other charges. I asked him to throw stalking in there, but he said he can't do anything with what we have. Flowers and candy with a few cards that aren't threatening at all isn't a crime. Unwelcome, yes, but not threatening. At least in the eyes of the law."

I chuckle. "The very reason you wanted out."

He shrugs. "The law is a great tool. But only when it's applied and applied correctly. Some things are too vague. Some too strict. And others simply have no business being enforceable laws. And while all that shit is happening, I'll always have a job protecting those that cops want to but can't."

"Lila's going to be fucking ecstatic."

"That's not all. Guess who hit Lila then ran?"

My eyes narrow. "Fuck. Tell me Daniel."

"Yep. I've been working with Caden. We finally got our test back from the crime lab in Dallas. The paint on my truck matches the same type of truck I caught on my dashcam before we got hit. That old 80's Dodge. It was the fucking dirt, though, that Caden picked up. Apparently, there are particular nutrients in it that match an expensive fertilizer shipped directly from Japan."

I raise an eyebrow. "And how'd you manage to match that to Daniel?"

"He was smart with Lila, the flowers, and all of the stalking, but he used his own credit card to get that fertilizer, which is being used in his own personal garden at his house. Some Japanese garden going in his backyard. We got a search warrant and found the smashed up truck in his fucking garage. Matched the paint on my truck to his. And the best part? His license plate matched the one I caught in my dashcam."

"I thought it was just a picture of a flag. Nothing else."

"It was. The flag, though, was interesting. Something I've never seen before. It's associated with a cult."

"If you tell me there's a cult after Lila, I might kick your ass."

He shakes his head. "Fuck no. He wanted to join them. They didn't want him."

"Cults lie."

Evan laughs. "Not this one, man. They're a cult, but not like you think. They worship Barbie. They think God is a woman, and fuck, maybe that's true." He shrugs. "They think her soul is in Barbie."

I just blink. "Dude. No. No fucking way."

He grins. "Daniel has a Barbie fetish."

I laugh. "Get the fuck off my property with that shit."

He laughs and pats my back. "He's going down for attempted homicide with a deadly weapon for the hit and run. We have a lot more evidence after the search that it was all planned. There's a list of charges. He's not going anywhere. I'm pretty sure one of our lovely State penitentiaries will make him up a nice room."

"As long as his roommate is a seven foot man named Butch, I'm good." I wink as he laughs again. I head for the turkey to check on it.

I'm glad we have someone like him on our side.

A couple of hours later, I'm just finishing setting up Thanksgiving dinner. I grin when I hear the fire engine backing into the bay. The entire station house smells mouthwatering. As soon as they step out of the truck, they're all going to be running up to our dining area.

As predicted, everyone comes running in with Nick leading the pack.

"God, that smells incredible."

"Clean up and dig in," I say with a grin. "Eat before my asshole brother puts you to work."

Elden laughs as he walks in. "There's a lot of shit to do. But I've been holding off. I'll make them work all the food off." He gives me a wink. It's exactly what I'd do.

As everyone starts to settle and bond over the meal, I make my exit. I have two more turkeys to cook and several people to help Lila prepare for. I usually host a few cookouts throughout the year for the firefighters, but this year, we wanted to do something more personal.

And with Lila by my side, I can't wait to get started.

Much later, after the sun has set and the bonfire is going strong, I grin at the people sitting or standing around talking and horsing around. Lila has a game of tag going with a couple of her bandmates and her backup singers as well as Evan. Lila's parents as well as mine are here. Keelan, Luke, Bentley, and Ashe, all from my crew are here.

And we've been joined by our team on Crew C. Estrella, their Captain, is having the time of her life in that tag match. Everyone else is interacting with other people who are here. All in all, I'm happy with the turnout.

Beau, Estrella's new Lieutenant who transferred from a department up in Kansas City, was talking to a few people today, but he's currently sipping a water and watching the flames of the fire.

I sit down next to him. "Enjoying our little slice of Heaven? Or are you missing Kansas City?" I take a long drink from the bottle of beer in my hand and stare at the flames in front of me.

Beau chuckles. "I am. It's a good change."

"I haven't heard anything bad about you, so I'm guessing you're fitting right in." I grin.

He grins back and glances at me before looking back at the bonfire. "Give it time." He takes a drink. "I even met someone I can't get out of my head."

"Ah. I see." I nod but stay quiet. I've learned to let people talk if they want to and leave them alone if they don't. It might be the reason so many from all crews find their way into my office at some point talking to me about something. It's like a right of passage.

As predicted, Beau leans forward. "Okay. So, I gotta tell someone.." He looks over his shoulder at me, a cocky grin spreading over his face. I make a gesture with my bottle to go ahead, but keep my eyes on the fire, giving him my own cocky smile. "I had one hell of a night with someone. He was fucking hot. Best night of my life. There may have been a cowboy hat involved. I don't know who the fuck he is. No name. Number. Just the memory of that night burned in my brain. I don't know if he even lives in town or anything. But damn. I can't get him out of my head. He was perfect in every way."

I bite my lip and take a drink. "Damn."

He leans back and laughs. "I know. Hottest night of my life."

I laugh. "Man. I don't know. Luke will stick his dick in any girl available, Nick can't seem to find a girl to keep his interest longer than a couple weeks, and then goes months before he tries again. And now we have you, who fell head over heels in lust during a one-night stand but forgot to get any details at all about said one-night stand."

Beau laughs. "It was definitely a good night. And absolutely lustful. Maybe we'll meet up again."

I grin. "Well, you definitely ain't Prince Charming. You don't even have a glass slipper to go on. All you got is the memory of a cowboy hat. Maybe Fate will drop him in your lap again."

Beau laughs again. "You really live up to that straight-shooting asshole reputation you have. I knew I'd like you."

"I live to serve."

He smiles and laughs again. "Appreciate the talk. Now, if you don't mind, that game of tag looks like it turned into a flag football game."

"Oh, I'm definitely down for that."

I finish off my beer and jog after Beau towards the cheers and squeals coming from the impromptu game. I watch as Lila catches the football I'm sure someone found in my garage, and then takes off towards the makeshift endzone. Just as she reaches it, I reach her. I pick her up and spin her around in a circle as she squeaks.

"Blake! Did you see? I did it!"

"I saw," I rumble against her neck. "But it's just turned into a real game, Miss America. And I choose you for my team."

I set her down and swat her ass as she laughs and takes off with the ball towards the middle of our yard. I laugh as Estrella points towards me and motions me over. She starts our game by calling out her first pick. I choose Lila for my team, and let the world fade away while we close out the night with our friends and loved ones.

This is the life I've always wanted.

I have no idea what the future has in store for us, but I look forward to every second of it.

I finally have everything I dreamed of.

I'm one lucky asshole.

The End

Piper Falls: Firehouse 49 Series

Available Now

Ignite My Fire by Melony Ann
Regain My Fire by Kindra White
Playing With My Fire by D.L. Howe
Fight My Fire by Darley Collins
Against My Fire by Anneke Boshoff
Relight My Fire by Louise Murchie
Harness My Fire by Ayana Lisbet
Quench My Fire by Havana Wilder

Other Books By Melony Ann
The Beautiful Dream Series

Available Now

Loving You
My Love, My Heart
Softening Lyric
Undercover Temptations
Captain Charming
Breaking Boundaries
Crashing Into You
Tactical Inferno
Ravishing Our Queen
Cherished By The Texan
Unveiling Our Passions

Box Sets Available

The Beautiful Dream Series: Box Set: Part 1
The Beautiful Dream Series: Box Set: Part 2

The Crane Family Series

Available Now

The Reluctant Mafia King
Sweet Lies
Billion Dollar Love Story
Be Mine
Protecting Her
Dangerously Forbidden Love
His Heart
Love In The Dark

The Deimos Trilogy

Available Now

Connor's Legacy
Aryan's Alpha
Kade's Redemption

Box Sets Available

The Deimos Trilogy

The Forbidden Temptations Series

Available Now

The Detective's Forbidden Temptation

The Lucinio Family Series

Available Now

Rising From The Ashes
The Player's Rebel
Encrypting My Heart

Let's Be Friends

Follow me on

Bookbub

Facebook

Goodreads

Instagram

Tik Tok

Visit my website
www.melonyannauthor.com

Subscribe to my newsletter and get a FREE never-seen-before NOVELLA
just for subscribers!
https://www.melonyannauthor.com/exclusive-content

Check out the Ignite My Fire playlist on You Tube!
https://www.youtube.com/playlist?list=PLGEiD5wbQmDd2AnL0gwC-8v-
0fXEIuTg3

Dedication

To the men and women who Ignite Our Fire.

Acknowledgements

Brad - The light in my darkness. I love you beyond words.

Laura - The calm in my storm. I love you beyond logic.

Jay - The safe harbor in my rough sea. I love you beyond understanding.

Ayana - Thank you for believing in me when so few did.

Anneke - Thank you for being the superwoman you are.

Jason - Thank you for being my inspiration.

To the Bookstagram Community.

To my family.

To all of those who believe in me and support me.

To all of those who don't.

Cover by: Carter Cover Designs

Edited by: Alyssa Skaggs

About Melony Ann

Melony Ann began writing short stories and poetry as a child. She continued honing her craft over the years until she took the plunge and began publishing her work, despite having severe anxiety.

Melony writes contemporary romance stories that are full of suspense and a lot of steam.

When she isn't writing, she is loving her family and working to make her life something she deserves.

Melony believes that if her writing can inspire just one person, then all of her hard work is worth it.

Her hope is that her writing allows each and every one of her readers to escape for a little while. To dive into a different world one book at a time.

www.ingramcontent.com/pod-product-compliance
Lightning Source LLC
Chambersburg PA
CBHW071923220626
47052CB00002B/436